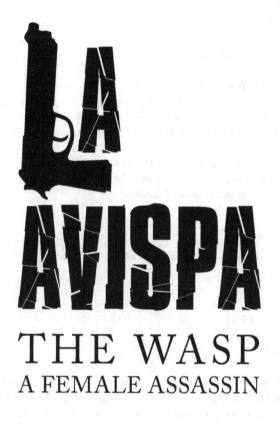

THE WASP
A FEMALE ASSASSIN

STANLEY FORD

iUniverse

LA AVISPA
THE WASP

iUniverse books may be ordered through booksellers or by contacting:

iUniverse
1663 Liberty Drive
Bloomington, IN 47403
www.iuniverse.com
844-349-9409

ISBN: 978-1-6632-2562-7 (sc)
ISBN: 978-1-6632-2563-4 (e)

Library of Congress Control Number: 2021915074

Print information available on the last page.

iUniverse rev. date: 07/23/2021

To
My Wife: Donna
My Sons: Gavin and Andrew
My friend: Captain Karell Wynter

Code name "Avispa." Juanita is beautiful and brutal and is driven by a burning passion that propels her from one hair raising situation to another.

A highly trained ex-Marine she is impacted by tragic events in her life that now motivates her to seek revenge and to fight the drug cartels of Mexico and Central America from the inside.

She is a natural at what she does and using all the skills developed she gets the mission done. Her lifestyle is commensurate with her chosen field, and she stays alive by outthinking and out maneuvering her rivals.

The story is told in graphic detail and insight as it takes you with her to several countries and into the heart of the cartels, on her quest as an assassin, to track down and terminate her targets with her deadly sting.

CHAPTER 1

The two speed boats circled the small, unarmed boat at high speed, peppering it with a fusillade of machine gun bullets. Circling like a pack of hyenas, they closed in on the defenseless craft for the kill. The scene that followed seemed to play out almost in slow motion as the bomb, lobbed from one of the speeding boats, found its mark and the small craft exploded, sending debris and body parts flying in all directions. As quickly as it happened, it was over and the speed boats fled leaving an eerie calmness accentuated by only an acrid smell, a few bits of debris, and little else.

The sudden contact of the tires of the aircraft on the runway jolted Juanita out of her nightmarish reminiscing that had become a part of her life. Ever since that day and that tragic incident her life had been impacted forever. She remembered the close-knit family she had; Mom would be busy in the kitchen fixing her culinary delights but would pause as she entered and offer her a taste of whatever she was preparing. Sometimes in jest Juanita would make a face and say, "yuck mom what is that" to that her mom would respond "It's what everybody will be eating tonight except you." Then she would flash one of her motherly smiles and give her a hug and a "now get out of my kitchen you little devil". Juanita also remembered her mom sitting with her and going over her schoolwork and encouraging her to do well as hard work will always pay off in the end. How well she remembered these oft repeated words by her mom, "Heights of great men reached and kept were not attained by sudden flight but they while their companions slept were toiling upward through the night." Juanita was always impressed by how wise her mom was although she only had minimal schooling. Mom was her teacher, nurse, confidant and source of inspiration. She also, remembered how when the time came and her mom could no longer help her with her High School work how it affected her mom for a while. It was only the kindness and love that Juanita showed that helped to ease the pain. It also helped when mom turned to helping the younger siblings with their work.

Juanita twisted again in the seat as memories of her father now flooded her mind. She remembered his last words to her. "Juanita you are going out into a great big world, but it is for you to control your world within that world, you can either limit your world or you can expand it". She remembered the walks with her dad to the nearby park and sometimes down to the beach. They would walk hand in hand and anyone looking on could see the bond and love between them.

Her entire family was a close-knit unit built on a foundation of love and respect for one another, they were in all respect a model family in their community and people respected them.

With memories of her brothers surging forward she cried herself into a fitful few minutes of sleep just before the aircraft tires hit the tarmac.

Such reminiscing would always end with a growing amount of anger and a vow that she would have her revenge. That was no way for an innocent law-abiding family, her family, to die.

Juanita Munir, code name La Avispa (The Wasp) had just arrived at the Donald Sangster International Airport in Montego Bay Jamaica aboard Delta Airlines flight 317 nonstop from Atlanta, Georgia. It is now 11:15 a.m. She had deliberately chosen this route to avoid flying directly out of her hometown of Orlando, Florida.

With her usual easy style and seductive smile, she quickly cleared Immigration and Customs and boarded the waiting hotel shuttle bus for the Rio hotel.

What was not apparent behind her brand name sunglasses was the coldness in her hazel brown eyes, a coldness that had developed over the years since the massacre of her family. The feeling had grown and become more intense as she internalized that traumatic day which in the end would propel her toward her present deadly profession. She was an assassin and a very efficient one.

On her way to the Rio Juanita sat quietly at the back of the bus and studied every feature of the landscape, while studiously avoiding any of the usual tourist chatter.

The bus arrived at the hotel and disgorged its passenger into the waiting cadre of bellhops and other hotel workers. She went quickly and was soon settled in her room on the sixth floor. She was always careful to request a room away from an outside corridor and close enough to an elevator, to avoid walking down a long hallway.

Having meticulously checked the room Juanita poured herself a single shot of vodka from the complimentary bar in the room and downed it in one gulp. She examined the glass for a moment as if trying to figure out some secret it might be hiding from her but finding none, she sat on the edge of the bed and gently lay back and closed her eyes.

After lunch it was time for her to explore the property in order to acquaint herself with its layout and to confirm that all was as portrayed in the map in her room and which she had meticulously studied. At about 3:30 p.m. she changed into bikini and with a recently purchased wrap thrown loosely around her she headed for the beach where the beautiful white sand and crystal-clear water waited expectantly to embrace her.

Juanita had an exquisitely well-toned body developed over years of dedicated physical training while in the military and later in the gym, which had become an integral part of her lifestyle. As she walked with that effortless catlike grace that is only achieved by the physically fit and self-assured; she could almost read the minds of the men who watched her go by, along with the thinly veiled envy of the other females who glanced at her and then threw sidelong glances at their men as if daring them to look. She was a knockout, and she knew it.

The sun began to set, slowly giving rise to a gentle breeze and a spectacular display of colors just above the Western horizon. It was not until after it had disappeared completely below the waves that Juanita replaced the top of her bikini, collected her belongings and headed back to the room. As she walked, she became aware of the phalanx of men who watched her every move. There were the bald pot-bellied ones, the once buff, now shriveled old bodybuilders, the young jocks, and the hen pecked. As varied as they were in appearance, so also were their professions, but she knew they all had one thing in common, lustful thoughts. They all wanted to seduce her.

Supper was room service then it was an early night. She had come to Jamaica for a very special reason but since she had not visited the island before, she decided to see as much of it as possible. To do that her reservation included one of the many tours offered by the hotel and she also wanted to be up early to take her customary five-mile run before breakfast and still be able to make the tour.

Breakfast was heavenly, replete with a variety of tropical fruits all grown on the island and therefore not subjected to most of the chemicals applied to fruits and vegetables produced in the more developed countries.

The tour got under way precisely at 9:00 a.m. The first stop was at the famous Green Grotto Caves in the parish of Saint Ann, then it was on to Dunn's River Falls. From there it was on to Dolphin's Cove where the more adventurous got their dreams fulfilled by swimming with and petting the dolphins.

Back at the hotel it was a steamy twenty minutes in the sauna, then supper, after which she went by the beach bar and ordered a margarita. While at the bar one of the islanders, who was also a guest at the hotel, struck up a conversation. Errol was from Kingston the capital of the island, located on its southern coast but he had traveled to Montego Bay, on the northwestern side of the island, on business. Upon learning this was her first visit to the island, he invited her out for a drive to show her around the town.

Montego Bay, along with Negril and Ocho Rios, are the three main tourist areas of the island and between them they share some of the best beaches and most popular attractions.

In recent times, however, Montego Bay has become infamous for what is known as the lotto scam. This is a criminal activity which involves the fleecing of unsuspecting persons out of millions of dollars each year. The scammers contact individuals mostly in the United States and convince them that they have won money, a house, or vehicles. The victim then must pay money for the transaction to be processed. Once the bait has been taken, however, the scammers make more and more demands on the victim, extracting as much as they can from them before finally cutting them loose.

The scheme is so popular and lucrative that it is not uncommon to see teenage boys driving the most expensive vehicles and constructing the most elaborate houses in some of the more affluent sections of the town or its outskirts.

This scheme has become so pervasive and embarrassing to the island that the police force has now put in place a special unit to deal with it. The government has also become quite aware of its potential to cripple the economic life of the country as foreigners become wary of doing business with local entities and so there is now an all-out thrust to deal with the problem. There are now ongoing discussions concerning changing some laws and introducing others in order to adequately arrest the perpetrators.

These activities and the corresponding upsurge in criminal activities prompted the government to come up with innovative ways of tackling the problem. One such measure was the passing of the Act that gave the Prime Minister the power to declare an area a Zone of Special Operations in order to tackle increased crime and volatility in the community. In essence those areas are subjected to a kind of State of Emergency in which the military and the police becomes much more visible as they carry out check points and conduct raids. Since its passing a number of areas of the country have been designated as such and there has been positive results in those areas. Montego Bay is one such area.

Errol and Juanita drove around for a while before ending up at the popular nightspot, Margaretville; there he had a few beers while she had one glass of wine and declared that as her quota for the night. As he enjoyed his beers, she noticed that his inhibitions began to fade, and he was becoming more amorous to the extent that her guard immediately went up and she decided to call it a night.

On arriving back at the hotel, he invited her to his room for a night cap, but the offer was politely declined. He obviously thought that was just her way of playing hard to get so he reached over and touched her exposed thigh in a gentle stroking motion. Her reaction was swift and brutal, and the speed with which he left her in the parking lot would have made any of his very athletic countrymen immensely proud, it would also give him time over the coming weeks to contemplate his mistake while waiting for his two broken fingers to heal.

The next day Juanita checked out early and left the hotel in the rental car she had booked the day before. The journey took her to the much talked about Negril area with its seven miles of white sand and its spectacular sunset as viewed from Rick's Café.

The drive to Negril, which is the most western tip of Jamaica, was quite pleasant except for the occasional crazy taxi man, or bus drivers who seemed to have a death wish as they barreled along the road, seemingly heading to some invisible fire. One local she spoke with about the taxis, very nonchalantly said "Oh you mean the missiles, that's what we call them". Juanita tried to mimic his native accent by responding "Dem crazy mon but no problem".

The time in Negril went quickly with the afternoon finding her at Ricks Café where she watched some adventurous souls go cliff jumping into the crystal-clear water below. That was topped off by the breathtaking sunset as the sun seemed to linger for a moment above the horizon, transforming it into a kaleidoscope of colors and then it was gone and the night shadows took over. As beautiful as the scene was, it left Juanita with a momentary feeling of sadness. That feeling was not conducive to socializing, so after a long walk on the beach, followed by a workout in the hotel's gym, it was supper and bed. During the walk along the beach, she reminisced on her army training and how at one point in my life she had begun to detest sunsets and dawns. This she realized had come from the incessant stand-to at maximum alert that was drilled into her while on field training. She now mused at how circumstances in her life had changed to the point that sunrise and sunset were now her favorite times of day. The sunset and night would cover her retreat when needed on some missions, while on other occasions the dawn would give her just the amount of light needed to get into position and prepare for the daybreak.

That night, before falling asleep, Juanita took out the local road map and studied it intently with the aim of getting a feel for the journey she would be undertaking the next day as she headed for the eastern end of this elongated island.

The journey from Negril to Port Antonio, affectionately referred to as Portie by the locals, covers two hundred and ninety-eight kilometers and could take as long as six hours. In order to make her 3:00 p.m. meeting she decided to head out immediately after breakfast. Not being one to take chances, she had factored in any unplanned eventuality such as bad weather, or an accident caused by one of the missile taxies or one of those lunatic bus drivers.

The journey somehow reminded her of some of those trips she had taken with her parents as they traveled from their home near the coast to visit with her maternal grandparents in the interior of the Dominican Republic. She remembered the lush vegetation, sometimes glistening in the sun with the overnight dew. Often there would be cattle grazing on the hillsides overlooking small fields of food crops planted by the local farmers. She remembered well on one occasion, watching a scrawny little dog taunting a very large bull in an open field. He would charge in and the bull would stomp a hoof and lower its head in anticipation but the dog would stop just short, run off in a wide circle then come charging in again. This continued for as long as they were visible from the vehicle in which she was traveling, and she remembered wondering how long it had been going on and how long it would continue.

The venue for the meeting in Port Antonio had been very carefully selected for its privacy and location away from the beaten path. The cottage selected was one of five on the property known as Blue Beyond, in the area of Snow Hill, some fifteen minutes west of the town of Port Antonio.

The cottages are perched atop a sheer cliff overlooking the sea and about five hundred meters from the main road. It was the ideal spot for the meeting with Pablo.

Upon arrival at the cottage, she let herself in with the key that had been delivered to her, in a sealed envelope by the desk clerk at the Rio hotel. She then quickly retrieved the Glock 17 pistol from a safe behind the bookcase in the hallway. A quick inspection of the interior of the cottage was carried out and as this was uneventful it was now time to do a quick sweep of the surrounding area and await her contact.

He arrived at exactly 3:00 p.m. and with the necessary authentication of identity completed, he entered, and they immediately got down to business.

Pablo Sanchez was a very well-built man in his mid forties with a slightly receding hairline and piercing eyes. From the cautious way he moved and his almost undetectable canvassing of the area, it was easy to guess that he had seen his fair share of adventure and excitement in his lifetime.

Satisfied that they were alone, Pablo started to explain his mission to Juanita in his heavily accented English. Quickly summing up the situation she began to address him in Spanish, which he, with visible relief was more than happy to do as his grasp of English was quite lacking in many respects and he knew it.

"Juanita" he said, "I represent a very powerful group of business men doing business in Guatemala." "The business has been doing quite well and is financially very stable." "Over the past few years, however, a certain Mexican drug cartel has been spreading its influence in that country and this is posing a problem for the organization."

What Pablo omitted to tell Juanita was that the cartel he was talking about was the very large and aggressive Zetas cartel, or that he represented their arch rival the Gulf Cartel.

"The main person involved in this incursion is a businessman by the name of Elan Morales Garcia." "He is being used by the cartel to buy into a wide range of businesses in Guatemala as the cartel seek to expand its influence in the region, with the intention of transforming it into a drug transshipment point."

Pablo went on to explain that at present Elan held interests in businesses ranging from farming to manufacturing, and transportation, which were the pillars of the fragile economy, and which posed a clear and present danger to the stability of the government. The businesses, he said are simply fronts for money laundering operations.

Pablo was very clever in the way he tied in the truth of what was happening in the region with her mission, while at the same time hiding his real objective. It was indeed true that the cartels had made an overly aggressive incursion into Central America. So aggressive in fact, that the President of El Salvador, Mauricio Funes had explicitly stated that combating organized crime in the region and in particular El Salvador, Guatemala and Honduras must be treated with priority. The alarming increase in crime was rapidly approaching a critical mass and in recent years those three countries had earned the dubious distinction of having the highest murder rates in the world.

Having outlined his scenario, Juanita's mission was presented to her in stark terms: "Juanita your mission is to eliminate Elan at the earliest possible time." Pablo reiterated that the mission would not only save the Guatemalan government from total collapse but would possibly save the lives of many Guatemalans. "Juanita, can you let me have your answer in twenty-four hours?" "Should you decided to accept, a half million dollars, will be paid immediately and an additional half million on completion." He assured Juanita that they had considered her professional standards and that there would be no repercussions should she decide against accepting the assignment. Juanita did not believe him.

Juanita sat quietly for about five minutes and when next she spoke it was only to confirm her acceptance of the mission and to lay down her ground rules.

He agreed to her conditions and assured her that by the time she got back to the USA the deposit would be in her account. It would be sent through a cartel operated shell company, as work done for the company as a consultant, in Jamaica. This he said would take some of the scrutiny off the source of funding by the bank in the USA.

As she showed Pablo to the door, she took an orange from the basket on the table and offered it to him. As he reached for it, she very casually said to him "very pretty on the outside but this one is really sour on the inside, be careful". Pablo seemed a bit stunned by her words but he only stared at her for a while then turned and walked away.

Juanita had promised herself that she would go hiking up in the Blue Mountains which she had heard so much about and which were almost outside the back door of the cottages at Blue Beyond, but something about this assignment and the fact that she had a bad feeling about Pablo was telling her to get the hell out of there as soon as possible and so she decided to leave the following morning.

The beach at the foot of the cliff below the cottage, was not ideal for swimming as it consisted mostly of large pebbles washed smooth over the years by the motion of the waves. It created a gentle rattling sound as each wave broke on the shoreline, then receded, only to be repeated a few seconds later. This created an almost hypnotic sound which, combined with the gentle breeze coming up the cliff, should have been enough to lull Juanita into a sound sleep. That was not to be. She spent the night in a restless sleep interspersed with flashbacks of her childhood.

Juanita often reflects on her early days growing up in the port town of Puerto Plata in the Dominican Republic. Her father worked on one of the fishing vessels which operated out of the port, while her mother stayed home and looked after the children. She was the middle child of five. There were two older brothers, a younger brother, and a sister. Those brothers, without knowing it, would play an especially important role in shaping her life and preparing her for military service. She would tag along with them as they went to the beach and on hikes into the interior and would even get involved in their rough and tumble unsupervised self defense training. There were many evenings when she would have to avoid her mothers' eyes because of bruises sustained in such frolics.

Juanita graduated from high school with relatively good grades and after trying to decide on a career, finally decided to go to the United States to further her studies. This was not a problem for her, as unlike her siblings she was born in the United States of America. It seemed fate had played a hand in her life even before she was born. Due to a life-threatening pregnancy with Juanita her mother's obstetrician had recommended that she seek the necessary expertise in Miami. This was done and Juanita was delivered in the United States. And so it was that on her eighteenth birthday Juanita left for the United States to fulfill her desire.

The University of Central Florida in Orlando was her choice, and she was quietly awed by its size and its offerings but after two semesters she became bored and restless. Then one morning without ever giving it any prior thought she found herself in the Marine Corp recruitment center filling out an application. It was to be a life changing decision.

Daybreak came as a welcome relief from her restless sleep; Forced to switch from her childhood reminiscing; she now focused on the journey ahead into Kingston from where she would board her flight to Orlando, Florida. The drive to Kingston along the narrow, winding country road was a pleasant yet scary experience. She had been through enough in her life up to this point, to not be scared easily; yet hugging the curves on the mountain roads was unsettling. Aside from the heavily laden trucks and the country buses which careened around blind corners at speeds that were more befitting the Florida turnpike, the drive was nonetheless pleasant. This was so, because of the lush greenery of the countryside, with mountains that seemed to rise directly out of the edge of the road on one side, and the river which ran alongside for most of the journey on the other. She allowed herself to take some small comfort in the research she had done, that stated there are usually more serious and frequent accidents along the four and six lane highways in other parts of the island, than on these winding country roads. This was possibly due to the fact that people took more chances on the multiple lane highways, but up here with the sheer cliffs and hairpin turns, there was a heightened sense of awareness.

That adventure behind her she made it to the airport in Kingston, and after clearing Immigration, ordered an ice-cold Red Stripe beer; the beloved local beer held in high regard by the islanders, and now making significant headway into the foreign market. The beer did the trick. She was back to being her totally composed self, and soon began to indulge in her favorite pastime. She would pick out individuals in a crowd and try to assess them and get inside their heads to figure out what they were thinking or what they would do next. Much of what was gathered came from looking at their eyes and body language. It was Pablo's eyes that had aroused her suspicion.

The flight was spot on time, and within two and a half hours was touching down in Orlando.

CHAPTER 2

The next three days were spent meticulously planning for her assignment which included a trip to Guatemala. This involved tying up arrangements with Pablo concerning the conduct of the mission. It was normal for her to operate as a team of three. A facilitator would make all the arrangements for travel, accommodation and the firearms drop; then a cleaner would go in after she had done the hit. The cleaner's job was to scour the area to remove any possible incriminating evidence, and in general cover her back. She was the trigger: it was her task to execute the mission. She is the assassin.

The mission this time, however, would be somewhat different. There would be no cleaner, at least not known to her and the facilitator would not be in on the plot. Instead, he was to be co-opted into the operation as an innocent participant. Most of the arrangements that would normally be taken care of by the facilitator were to be handled by her and she was to cover her own withdrawal.

Again, that warning bell began ringing about Pablo and his trustworthiness or lack thereof.

After checking and double checking the arrangements, she was ready for the trip. The itinerary would take her from Miami to Belize City then from Belize City to Guatemala City and finally by road to the town of Antigua.

The flight aboard Tan Air from Miami was quite full of mostly tourists, and so she blended in well and even struck up a conversation with Maurice, a very clean cut jovial young man who turned out to be a Navy diver. He was going to Belize to link up with some buddies, and as a group they would explore the coral reefs which lie just off the coast of Belize, and which are said to be some of the best preserved and pristine reefs left to be enjoyed.

When the flight landed in Belize City, Maurice told her where he was staying and expressed his desire to see her again, if she would contact him on her return from Belmopan. Not wanting to disclose her true destination she had told him she would be going to Belmopan to conduct research on the Mayan culture in the surrounding region.

Belmopan was developed as a replacement city for Belize City itself when the latter was almost demolished by Hurricane Hattie in the early 1960s. Although many government offices moved there it did not replace Belize City and it was not uncommon to have persons still living in Belize City and commuting to work in Belmopan daily.

As she did not intend to spend much time in Belize City, she headed directly to the car rental agency to collect the vehicle she had booked and was on her way. She drove to Belmopan then doubled back to Belize City where she stopped just long enough to purchase a few items in a craft store and to buy a cold drink. Then it was back to the airport for the onward journey to Guatemala. Now looking more like a tourist and hoping she would not run into Maurice. Had she done so, however, she already had a cover story to tell him. In her line of business survival depends on thinking fast and always having a plausible cover story.

The trip from Belize to Guatemala City was sufficiently long to give her time to rehearse and rehearse again and again in her mind the job that lay ahead. It does not matter how many of these missions are under the belt, the operative is constantly reminded that something can go terribly wrong, and that one slip could end their life. As she had no intention of transiting into the next life just, yet she continued to rehearse her plans.

Juanita thought about her accommodation, and the safety of her weapon, her final preparation for executing the mission, and her exit strategy. She also thought about the confidentiality of the person who would be keeping the weapon, and finally her mind flashed back to Pablo and the gnawing doubt she had about him.

Aside from the normal turbulence associated with the warmth and corresponding convection currents in that part of Central America during the summer months, the flight aboard the Dash 8 aircraft was relatively smooth and the landing was equally smooth.

On exiting the aircraft, she was hit by a blistering blast of hot air which almost sent her souvenir straw hat, which she had purchased in Belize City, flying. Had it not been for her lightning-fast reflexes, she might have had a merry chase across the tarmac to retrieve it.

Immigration and Customs were cleared without fanfare and soon she was on her way to pick up the rental vehicle for the journey to the town of Antigua and the villa she had booked.

The town of Antigua, Guatemala is roughly southwest of Guatemala City and is approximately two hours by road cut through the lush forest. In some areas the jungle gives way to sheer cliffs along the road and some caution is required while motoring along.

On arriving in Antigua, she was instantly struck by its almost rustic beauty. It was as if time had stood still and was just now relaxing its grip on the town. The streets were beautifully paved with cobble stones and there were little shops everywhere mingled in with beautiful old Spanish style buildings and cathedrals. Overshadowing the towns like three giant sentinels standing guard are the volcanoes Agua, Fuego and Acatenango; renowned for their beauty and boasting the distinction of being the world's most photographed volcanoes.

Regardless of its beauty and history, there is an undercurrent of prejudice and suspicion which permeates this otherwise tranquil area. The native inhabitants are regarded with some disdain by the Spanish Caucasian population and as a result the resentment simmers much like the volcanoes, which could blow someday with catastrophic results.

Juanita went directly to the villa but after an hour she went back into the town to take in some of the scenery and to properly orientate herself. She noted the location of the police station, the rental car companies and the area where she should go the following day to retrieve her firearm for the mission.

It was times like these and situations such as this, that made her grateful for her mixed Hispanic background. With jet black hair, hazel eyes and dark skin she was more readily accepted by the natives. It did not seem to matter to them that she stood five feet nine inches, which made her approximately five inches taller than their average height and the topic of discussion and light-hearted joking.

Having satisfied herself that she had seen all she needed to Juanita returned to the villa and made a phone call to Pablo to let him know she had arrived.

The next day Juanita collected the deadly .50 M82A1 Barrett snipers rifle complete with AN/PVS-10 optic sight, from Angel La Bron the owner of the small hardware store in the town of Antigua. Angel's store was located a few blocks from the Grand market, famous for its tradition of haggling over the price of every item available for sale. The box containing the rifle was labeled as survey equipment and was addressed to Denise Truman from the firm Global Mapping Limited. Angel was a very affable man in his fifties and fit the basic profile of just about every man in the area. He was short of stature with jet black hair a ready smile, and friendly eyes. Once he was presented with the false identification in the name of Denise, he flashed his special grin which he apparently kept for special occasions such as this when he met foreigners.

Juanita is often taken aback by the innocence of persons like Angel and frequently wonder if they have the slightest concept of the cruel mysterious world that exists just outside their door and in which they sometimes become unwitting accomplices without having any inkling they are doing so.

That night as she examined the weapon in the seclusion of the small villa she had rented, just on the outskirts of Antigua, she tuned into the local radio station. As she listened somewhat casually to the radio, she heard the news item of the businessman who had died in an automobile accident on his way home. At first it meant nothing to her except the fact that another human had fallen victim to the ever-growing list of persons who meet their demise in motor vehicle accidents. She kept on inspecting the weapon. Suddenly she was jolted upright when she heard the name of the driver and the name of his business establishment. Angel La Bron somehow had driven off the road and over the precipice as he had made his way home to his wife and children.

Angel had unknowingly stepped into that cruel and sinister world, and his foray had been short-lived and innocent. He died in a flaming wreck at the bottom of a gorge.

It is not normal for Juanita to be touched by death or tragedies. She had lived with them all her adult life and had even created quite a number herself, but Angel's death somehow resonated with her. Maybe it was because it again reinforced the feeling that her clients were not to be trusted or taken lightly as they played to their own set of rules. Juanita was convinced they had murdered Angel.

The inspection of the weapon completed; she was satisfied that it was in the same mint condition as the last time she handled it just prior to leaving for Guatemala.

Elan Morales Garcia was a wealthy man who enjoyed his lifestyle and was pleased with his achievements. He had spent the last twenty years building a small empire within Guatemala and he was now ready to enjoy it to the maximum. His palatial dwelling was the center piece of his farm, which was carved out of the countryside some ten miles to the northwest of the town of Antigua. The area immediately around the house was beautifully landscaped, with a palm lined driveway, and a variety of tropical fruit trees. There was a stable which boasted some of the most expensive horses in Central America. The layout was complete with an Olympic size swimming pool and a tennis court.

After working for several years as an accountant, Elan became disenchanted with his monotonous lifestyle and opted for something more exciting and financially rewarding. Capitalizing on his knowledge of alcoholic drinks gleaned from the large distribution company he had worked with for over fifteen years, he decided to try his hand in getting bootleg liquor into the United States. It was not long before he linked up with a member of the Gulf cartel in Mexico and soon, he was supplying them with a variety of products which they would filter across the border into the United States. His luck seemed to be going well as the Gulf cartel although heavily involved in the trafficking of cocaine and marijuana into the United States, had a long history in bootlegging dating back to the 1930s. With Elan being able to provide a reliable supply he was seen as an asset to the organization.

In a noticeably short time, he was totally embraced by the cartel and began to realize his lifelong dream to break the bond of poverty that had surrounded him as a child.

As Elan began to see the results of his new venture, he quickly made good on one of this fervent promise to his mother; that he would one day make her comfortable. Not only had he accomplished that goal, but he was now also very comfortable himself and lacked nothing.

For the past six months, every morning at sunrise Elan would play tennis with his nine-year-old daughter Maria whom he adored and who adored him in return. The past year had seen them bonding even closer, following the death of his wife Analeida. She had died in an airplane crash while on her way back from San Pedro Cay, off the coast of Belize. There was much speculation about the crash and some persons were convinced that he had arranged it.

It seemed that for some time Analeida had been pressuring him to break ties with members of the drug cartel that he was so deeply imbedded with, and although he would solemnly promise her that he would, nothing changed. Things had come to a head a year ago and she told him she was leaving. He had pleaded with her and promised that he would do as she requested. He then suggested she take a few days' vacation in San Pedro while he sorted everything out. It was on the way back from her vacation that the twin-engine Baron Beechcraft airplane developed engine problems and crashed in an open field in Belize, between Belize City and Belmopan. All on board perished.

Elan walked onto the tennis court and began going through his usual warm up routine, which consisted of a few laps around the court and some stretching exercises. He was totally unaware that he was filling the telescopic sight fitted to the sniper rifle being cradled in Juanita's arms and that the cross hair was following every move of his head.

Juanita had selected her spot well on her reconnaissance conducted the day before. The spot was at the edge of the tree line, which was some twelve hundred meters from the tennis court. It was on a small mound with ample ground vegetation and a canopy of leaves from the overhead trees. She blended in well in the camouflaged suit she had chosen.

The morning sun was just making its appearance and already the tropical heat could be felt. The perspiration started to trickle down the center of Juanita's back and she was glad she had worn the bandana around her head and under her baseball cap. The bandana kept the perspiration that formed on her forehead, from making its way down into her eyes.

Her body was almost motionless as she did her final adjustment for wind and elevation. Her index finger caressed the trigger. A final check on the wind and the target's anticipated movement, then a gentle squeeze.

Elan had made the same tragic mistake that so many others had. Just as things were going so well, he allowed greed to get the better of him. It started on one of his frequent trips into Guatemala City when he was approached by a member of the Zetas cartel. The contact told him that he had come to the attention of the cartel, and they were convinced that he would fit in very neatly with their business plans for Guatemala. They assured him it would be tremendously profitable.

After two additional meetings and the mysterious disappearance of two of his shipments, he contacted the cartel's man and arranged a meeting.

It was outlined to him that the Zetas cartel was expanding into Central America in countries such as Guatemala, Honduras, El Salvador, and Belize and to that end they needed reliable persons in each country to facilitate their moves.

He was to be responsible for negotiating the purchase of lands and buying into other legitimate businesses. He would buy into everything including farms, manufacturing companies and the transport system. All this to strengthen the organization and facilitate both money laundering and the cocaine trade.

Elan realized that he was now in much deeper waters than he had bargained for but the potential power and the financial gains overcame his better judgment. That was to be a tragic mistake. He was about to turn his back on his old partner, the Gulf cartel and that would not augur well for a lengthy sojourn here on earth.

At that split second, just as the trigger reached the point of no return Juanita saw Maria running towards her father with tennis racket in hand. Elan's head exploded in front of her as the .50 caliber warhead found its mark.

Juanita saw Maria freeze for a moment then crumpled to the ground like a rag doll. There was no time however to dwell on Maria's status as she had to take care of Elan's two bodyguards. The one standing just behind him on the court was the first to go after which she dispatched the other who had been standing at the rail of the gazebo a short distance away. Like Elan the guards were dispatched with such precision they were clueless as to the source and means of their demise.

Juanita had just killed the man who had sat next to her the night before and had offered her a drink, and she had done it in full view of his daughter.

As a rule, she never contacts her intended victims before eliminating them and so it was quite by accident that she had met Elan.

Another realization also struck her as she drove away from that scene; she suddenly realized that the two bodyguards who had just been taken out were not the ones she had seen with Elan the day before. That made her begin to wonder just how many more there were and how loyal they were to him.

The day before the hit Juanita had gone to the marketplace in Antigua to do what all tourists do: purchase souvenirs. To her surprise she quite enjoyed haggling with the vendors and felt elated when she could talk them down from their original price even by a mere fraction of it. As enjoyable as it was, it had left her somewhat thirsty and a little drained, so she had gone into a nearby café for a drink. She ordered a fruit juice and took a seat at a table in a corner. The café was dimly lit and there were very few patrons, but she did notice one gentleman sitting alone at a table near the corner she had chosen. It took only a few minutes for her eyes to fully adjust, having just come in from the bright sunshine outside. As they adjusted, she must have done a double take, as she recognized the gentleman next to her was none other than Elan Morales Garcia, her intended target. Although not known to show emotion, something must have happened to catch Elan's eye, as he asked her if she was alright. Without hesitating she said yes and made the excuse that it was the sudden change from the heat outside to the cool atmosphere in the café. He said he understood, and that it was for that same reason he had come in just to relax for a moment. He then went on to say how cooped up he felt in his vehicle and that he just had to get out and stretch his legs. He said that the heat had got the better of him, so he had come in for a drink, and to relax for a while.

While he spoke Juanita noticed two men, who were armed, standing near the entrance door and glancing ever so often in their direction.

After chatting for a few minutes about her shopping expedition, he offered to buy her a drink. Juanita politely declined his offer and told him she had to be on her way. His parting remark was to be very prophetic. "I think we will meet again, one day soon".

The words came back to Juanita as she quickly gathered up the rifle and her other equipment and prepared for the very circuitous route she had taken from the spot where the rental vehicle was left.

The journey back to the villa was without incident. It would be some time before the news got to the police and they were able to mobilize. Juanita made two brief stops on the way; one to stash the rifle at a pre-arranged spot where it would be picked up and put on its very clandestine journey back to where it would be stored until it was next required. The other was to return the rental vehicle. After she returned that vehicle, she preceded a short distance down the road to another rental company and got a new one.

It was while driving back to the villa that Juanita was suddenly struck by the enormity of what she had just done. She had just killed a man in full view of his daughter. Despite her training and the hardened persona, she had developed this hit touched a chord that she might have thought had long died in her. Her mind took her back to her childhood days, playing with her father, running around and laughing with wild abandon and not a care in the world. Suddenly she was Maria and Elan was her dad and he had just had his head blown off in full view of her. For a moment she felt a shiver through her body as a wave of emotion swept through her, she felt unclean, guilty and remorseful for what she had just done and what she had become.

That night, for the first time in many years Juanita felt vulnerable. Not only did she feel vulnerable, but she found herself thinking of Maria and the trauma she had experienced that morning when she saw the head of her father explode in front of her like a water melon. The thoughts quickly dissipated however and soon she was in a very restful sleep.

Juanita had no idea that things were about to take a most troubling turn in the days ahead.

Juanita was up at the crack of dawn and headed for the airport in Guatemala City. At the airport, she went to the cafeteria and ordered a light snack before boarding the flight back to Belize City.

Sitting in the cafeteria enjoying her shuco and a coca cola she noticed a tall well-dressed Caucasian man sitting at a nearby bar. He was later joined by another man who appeared to be of Hispanic origin. They did not seem to have noticed her as she entered the cafeteria, but she had no doubt in her mind that the Hispanic gentleman was one of those who had been standing by the door in the café the day she met Elan. Juanita watched them for a while and at an opportune time, changed her position to an even less obvious one but one from which she could still observe them.

Both men chatted for about ten minutes, then the Hispanic one left and made his way out to what looked like a private aircraft parked on the tarmac. The other gentleman left the building soon after and went into an exceptionally large, heavily tinted SUV type vehicle, and drove away.

Unbeknown to her, there was also a third man in the cafeteria; he did not interact with the others, and he remained behind after they had left.

Later she learned that no sooner had she boarded her flight than he was on the phone giving the other two details of her flight into Belize City.

CHAPTER 3

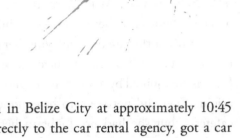

The flight touched down in Belize City at approximately 10:45 a.m. and Juanita went directly to the car rental agency, got a car then made a booking at one of the beach front hotels which lines the city's shore.

She did her usual check of the hotel room to ensure that she was the only occupant as she was not in the mood to be surprised. On being satisfied that the room was empty and that the locks worked on the door she proceeded to make herself comfortable sitting on the balcony which overlooked the swimming pool and the turquoise waters of the Caribbean Sea beyond.

Possibly a combination of the pull from the sea and the thought of Maurice the Navy diver having all that fun frolicking in the water. Whatever it was, she soon found herself donning a swimsuit and heading down to the beach.

The water must have been about seventy-six degrees Fahrenheit and it enveloped her in its embrace like a lover who craved her presence. Juanita enjoyed its every touch and gentle swaying motion, as it seduced her with its warmth and gentleness.

After about an hour in the water she had had enough of the sea's gentle embrace and headed back to the room. On entering the room, she instantly moved in a cat like motion to the other side near the balcony and away from the door. Juanita had detected the very faint smell of a man's cologne. In the blink of an eye, she had also noticed that one of her two shoes, that she had left at the side of the bed was out of place. It had been pushed slightly further under than the other. Although there was no one presently in the room, she called the front desk and requested a change, nevertheless.

Having had a possible intruder in her room, however, she had no intention of staying there that night and as soon as it was dark, she planned to move elsewhere, and would only return the next morning to pay the bill and get her stuff.

Maurice, although diving and taking in the local scenery with his friends, found himself thinking about Juanita and how much he wanted to see her again. Quite possibly it was his telepathic transmissions that were resonating with Juanita because she found herself thinking about him too.

It had been a long time since Juanita had found herself so taken in by anyone, as she had deliberately insulated herself from such emotions as falling in love or forming any close attachments. Something was happening however, and she could not fully grasp what it was. She had often thought to herself how frivolous those movies were, about people in her line of work hopping in and out of bed with every pretty face or handsome man they came across. The reality was, her world was a very cold and lonely one, cloaked in suspicion. This world of hers prevented her from dropping her guard enough to make her vulnerable to the intimacy of romantic relationships.

After enjoying a late lunch of freshly caught grilled fish, an abundance of vegetables and baked potatoes; she could not resist the urge anymore, so she made a call to Maurice. "Hi Maurice, do you have any plans for later, or would you like to hang out with me?"

"Juanita I cannot think of anything better that I would like to do than hanging out with you."

"In that case it's settled I will meet you at your hotel at about 8:00PM"

She could feel the excitement building up in her as it got closer to the time of their meeting she could hardly wait for nightfall. And she could hardly believe what was happening with her emotionally.

On seeing her Maurice was thrown in a mild state of shock. "Wow! Juanita, you look fabulous, where have you been hiding all my life."

"You can wipe that silly smile off your face my good man I bet you say that to all the girls you try to charm and sweep off their feet." "Thanks for the compliment, however, I had almost forgotten what that felt like."

Maurice then introduced her to some of his friends, after which they headed to one of the local restaurants for dinner.

Over dinner they shared many stories about their military life and as they did the bond seemed to tighten between them. Juanita found herself more relaxed than she could remember in a long time.

At close to midnight, they decided it was time to go, so they drove back to his hotel. Once there, he parked his vehicle, and they went by the bar in the hotel for a nightcap. Maurice then asked for the keys to her rental and told her to remain in the lobby as he brought it around from the parking lot. As she gave him the keys, she looked him straight in the eyes and asked, "Are you for real?" He responded, while returning her gaze "Time will tell." She then squeezed his hand, in a not-so-subtle show of affection and appreciation, as she gave him the keys. In a minute he was gone, and she stood shaking her head in a perplexed mood of anticipation and excitement.

When it came, the entire hotel was shaken to its foundation, then here was a deathly silence, followed by screams and persons running about. There was no mistaking it, the sound came from the parking lot and it sounded like a large bomb had gone off. Juanita was one of the first to arrive on the scene and she looked on in utter disbelief at the mangled wreck of the vehicle she had rented and was supposed to be in. All at once time stopped and everything seemed to move in slow motion. Just like that Maurice was gone but she realized that the fate Maurice had met was really intended for her. She made a silent vow there and then.

Someone would die horribly for this.

Juanita was forced to spend an extra day in Belize while being grilled by the local police who were desperately trying to put the pieces together. In the end they found nothing to incriminate her, and she was allowed to go. Before leaving, she was able to get one especially important bit of information; the suspect in the bombing was Elias Gulern, a former bodyguard of Elan Morales Garcia and now an associate of Manuel Ortiz.

The murder of Maurice brought back vivid memories of her family. She remembered how while out on Basic Training in the field with the Marines she had been picked up by a rather stiff First Sergeant and driven directly back to the base Chaplain. On arriving at the Chaplain's office her heart sank, as by now she had come to learn that those calls were normally the prelude to being informed of some tragedy. Not in her wildest dream, however, could she have imagined that she was about to be told of the death of her mother, father and two younger siblings.

Following the meeting, Juanita was sedated and hospitalized for three days, after which she received counseling and was granted leave to go home to continue grieving with what remained of her family.

Arriving home in the Dominican Republic, she learnt the grizzly details of her family's demise. Her father had rented a boat from one of his close fishing associates, for the purpose of going out on a night cruise off the North coast of Puerto Plata. It was his wife's birthday and he wanted to do something special with her and the two young ones. The story from there on is somewhat confusing, as there were no eyewitnesses left to tell exactly what happened on that terrible night. What was pieced together conjured up a picture of something that had gone terribly wrong. From a radio transmission which was intercepted by the Coast Guard of the Dominican Republic, there were frantic calls from the vessel being operated by her father. He was screaming that they were being attacked by unknown assailants in two high speed boats. The word later circulating in the Puerto Plata area, was that it was a case of mistaken identity and that the attackers had mistaken the boat for one that had recently rammed one of their drug boats and had made off with a large amount of cocaine which was destined for Barbados and onward to Europe.

After the murder of her family, she returned to the Marines a cold and angry person who spent most of her free time alone. Mistake or not, someone would pay dearly. Realizing that in order to fulfill her vow for revenge she had to improve certain skills. She threw herself into her shooting and field skills with new vigor and focus. It was not long before it was recognized by her instructors, who encouraged her to join the full-bore shooting team on the base and do competitive shooting. Things were going in the right direction as far as her future plans were concerned.

Juanita looked up and down the line of her fellow graduates and felt a sense of satisfaction. They felt ready to take on the world. Yes, they had come a long way. Friendships had been established and bonds created that only those who have undergone the rigors of unrelenting training, total exhaustion, and the comfort of a helping hand would ever understand. For Juanita, however, friendship existed around her but did not embrace her and it got even worse after the death of her family.

As she stood there in the bright winter sun, she recalled snippets of her training and how these had tested her. As she blinked her eyes, she again felt the cold wind ripping into her throat like razors and wondered just what had possessed her to take on military training in the middle of winter at Paris Island, South Carolina. She recalled the concerns of her family who had advised her that the training was rough enough without adding the dimension of cold to it. They reminded her that she was a tropical girl and not accustomed to cold and snow. She had laughed at their concern; what she had not said was that she felt herself to be in superior condition to the Americans. Yes, she had grown up in a different world and felt she could outperform her peers in all quarters. It was not long, however, before she began to have her doubts, she remembered how the slim instructor with the short afro and sculptured body had whizzed by her the first day out. She cursed her and prayed that she would fall or break a leg, anything to slacken the pace. Nothing however, eased the pace and with gritted teeth she plowed on.

The run to the range was the second run of the morning. Earlier they had been awakened at 04:30 by the Drill Sergeant and had to run four consecutive laps around the football field before doing their regular calisthenics. A quick shower had followed, then the monkey bars before breakfast and now this run to the range.

At the range they were issued live ammunition and in groups of fifteen, taken to the firing line where they were given last minute instructions. Over the loudspeaker she heard the voice, "Ready on the left, ready on the right, ready on the firing line." There was a slight pause, then the command: "You may commence firing". Targets popped up at random, fifty yards, one hundred yards, and two hundred yards. She had to be constantly adjusting in order to zero in on each new target with her M16 rifle. Initially she had braced herself for some sort of impact and had winced just at the point of squeezing the trigger. Feeling none, however, she had relaxed, and now fired with ease at each new target.

As her mind drifted from the firing line, it moved to the early days and the feeling of isolation as they were not allowed to go home. She recalled the girls who had gone absent without leave (AWOL) and had to be brought back by the Military Police. She had never been tempted to go AWOL, perhaps because she realized that her home was a world away from this horrible place and because she was never a quitter.

She remembered the Crucible, that final test which was conducted in the last week of training. During the Crucible, the recruits were subjected to field training and simulated war situations, food and sleep deprivation and forty-mile hikes. It was not unusual for recruits to hallucinate and do crazy things during this final last push.

She was brought back to reality by the sounding of the band as they tested their instruments. She listened halfheartedly and was again lost in her memories.

The Drill Sergeants had been rough, and she was at first confused by the seeming callousness of their approach. She, however, began to appreciate their motivation when she had a brief conversation with the young sergeant Carter. He had explained to her that it was their aim to keep them alive, to ensure that there would be fewer body bags heading home from the battlefield. To accomplish this, he had explained, meant pushing them to their limit and beyond; showing them no mercy, as the enemy would be singular in his intent to destroy them. The enemy, he pointed out, was even now studying their training, dedicating himself to be better and to be able to kill as many of her teammates as he could. This talk had inspired her to do better and from then on, her training took on a more personal approach and urgency. She kept on envisaging her enemy testing in a similar mode, with one aim to kill her and what she represented.

As she worked to improve her skills, she fell under the scrutiny of her training cadre who noted her resolve and took a personal interest in helping her to excel.

She felt a hand on her shoulder and looked around to see Betty smiling with her, she gave her a thumb's up, but was stoic as Betty grinned from ear to ear. She remembered a different Betty, a cheerful, slightly overweight girl who had fainted during their first overnight hike. She had to be taken back to the billets in an ambulance and had spent the next two days recuperating. No one felt that she would have made it but under the guidance of her drill Instructor (DI), she had slowly emerged into the confident person now standing behind her and giving her a thumb's up. Juanita was still unsure how she had let Betty into her closed world; a world that had been created by the death of her family. Betty and Juanita were opposites in so many ways, Betty was a cheerful chatty person who saw life as a big joke and had on more than one occasion, remarked that she had joined the marines to lose weight. "Cheaper than a spa" was her favorite line. Behind the chattiness and laughter however, Juanita had discovered a brain and an inquisitive nature. Simple answers never satisfied her and her constant questioning at times annoyed the DIs, but they answered, nevertheless. It was from her that Juanita had learned about calculating for wind and elevation, as this had been lost on her in the classroom during the early weapon's training lectures. Once she had got the hang of it, her shooting improved by leaps and bounds and soon she was amongst the five top shooters in her platoon. Betty also provided information on the wars fought by the corps, their history, and areas of deployment. Her knowledge seemed to have no bounds as she rambled from politics to small wars, and even the drug cartels of Columbia and Mexico. It was the latter that always captured the attention of Juanita and although she would seem not to care and did not ask any questions, she was taking it all in.

Betty hoped that she would be stationed as an embassy guard in an exotic country. Juanita just wanted to serve her time and get out, she had other plans.

The band again started up and Juanita looked up to see the colors being unfurled and the Drill Instructors and officers lining up in front of the formation. As the band sounded and she looked at the hundreds of fellow graduates from other training cycles, she felt surely, they were invincible. A surge of pride enveloped her, and she braced her shoulders. It was over, this was the final moment. A sudden feeling of emptiness soon overcame her however, as she looked around at the families and friends of other marines but there would be none there for her. She would receive medals and awards for her marksmanship and leadership qualities but her mixed emotions greatly overshadowed what should have been a moment of great happiness.

They had come a long way since the early uncertain days of their arrival, the terror of early morning wake ups, the ever-present monkey bars, the mud, and the long hikes. It had separated the fit from the unfit and those who remained felt confident in their achievement and ability to close with and kill the enemy.

CHAPTER 4

When President Felipe Calderon of Mexico unleashed the military on the drug trafficking gangs, it had almost the exact opposite effect he had anticipated. Instead of dismantling the cartels, it forced them to consolidate in order to survive. This not only strengthened them, but it saw the emergence of five major cartels which would soon push the number of persons murdered to over forty thousand in five years from 2006 to 2011.

Three of these cartels were the Gulf, Los Zetas and Ciudad Juarez cartels.

The Gulf Cartel was founded by Juan Nepomuceno Guerra in the 1970s and was then one of the largest drug trafficking groups operating in Mexico. Guerra himself had a long history of bootlegging into the United States and so when the decision was made to go into drug trafficking, he already had a well-established illegal network in operation. It soon became actively involved in the movement of cocaine, marijuana, heroin and methamphetamine into the USA.

The cartel was based in Matamoros, Tamaulipas on the coast of the Gulf of Mexico. In February of 2010 the Zetas, which was the armed wing of the Gulf cartel, broke away. Since then, they have been locked in deadly turf wars in the state of Tamaulipas and two other northern border states, Nuevo Leon and Coahuila. The fight with the Zetas forced the Gulf cartel into a strategic alliance with its sworn enemy, the Sinaloa cartel, with whom it fought brutally for control of Tamaulipas in 2004-05, as well as with former rival La Familia cartel.

The Zetas cartel is considered the most violent and ruthless criminal organization in Mexico. Made up of former Special Forces troops, it is highly organized, well armed and well equipped. It is known for its brutal tactics, which include beheadings, torture and indiscriminate slaughter. This cartel is highly suspected in the August 2010 killing of 72 migrant workers whose bodies were found dumped in a mass grave in Tamaulipas state near the U.S. border. Some suspect Los Zetas was also behind the Monterrey casino attack in 2011 in which some 52 persons died and in the attack on a farm in Guatemala where 27 persons including children were massacred. The group is known to have influence over the security forces, which has enabled it to carry out brazen attacks on police stations and other high-profile government targets. It controls much of the Gulf coast and has access to trafficking routes from Central America.

The Ciudad Juarez cartel operates out of the northern border town of Ciudad Juarez, just across from El Paso Texas. It straddles a highly fancied trafficking point and one of the most violent cities in the country. Its bloody rivalry with the Sinaloa cartel led to almost 6,500 deaths in Ciudad Juarez between December 2006 and December 2010. This accounted for 19 per cent of all homicides in that period. The cartel is allied with the Zetas and Beltran-Leyva and is sometimes called the Vicente Carrillo Fuentes Organization, after its leader. The armed wing of the cartel is known as "La Linea" and it often recruits and trains beautiful young women as "sicaras" (hired assassins). It was this cartel that had wooed Juanita on her discharge from the Marines and eventually won her over. Let no one be fooled into thinking, however, that it was the convincing words of her recruiter that won her over; she had her own motive.

Ever since the murder of her family by suspected drug cartel members, Juanita had been seething with revenge and throwing all logical reasoning aside she had decided that if it meant that she had to go in amongst them to do the most damage, then she would. Having been accepted, she felt that she was now one step closer to realizing her dream. A dream which would give her the chance to target those involved in the murderous drug trade, and anyone else who supported them. The latter would simply be collateral damage.

Juanita went through an intense period of indoctrination, which emphasized the need for confidentiality and loyalty to the group. The loyalty point was forcibly driven home by the numbers of executions of persons, who were suspected of crossing the cartel, that she had to watch and participate in.

Following this phase, she was given assignments moving weapons from one location to another or negotiating drug sales with some influential persons and some low-ranking government officials in Mexico. Finally, one day she had audience with a high-ranking member of the cartel who congratulated her and informed her that they were now confident that she was ready for the role in the organization for which she had been recruited. Two weeks after that meeting, she was assigned her first job.

Her assignment was to eliminate the head of the police unit in a little town, some twenty miles from Ciudad Juarez. To accomplish her mission, she traveled to the region and did a detailed study of the movement of the officer. When she felt sure that she had all the variables covered, she returned to Ciudad Juarez and made her plans to return two days later. She chose a spot along one of the narrow country roads which led from the little town and ran past the home of the officer. The road selected ran parallel to another somewhat larger road and was separated by approximately two hundred meters of woodland. She had her appointed driver drop her off at a preselected spot on the side of the main road, then she made her way through the woods to the spot she had selected for the hit. Once there, she did her preparation and started her wait.

The wait was not long, as her target was a creature of habit and arrived just about the time she had predicted. As the car came around the slight bend in the road, she could clearly see the face of the driver. She squeezed the trigger. The car swerved to one side, then the other and finally ended up in a ditch; she chambered and fired one more round into the slumped body. It was time to get out quickly but just then another vehicle caught her sight. It stopped and two men got out quickly both carrying Ak-47 rifles. The one who was in the passenger's seat opened with a short burst. She could hear the crack of the bullets as they whizzed by her. Juanita went to ground behind an old tree stump and got off one quick shot. It found its mark and the man went down. By this time, the other man was just topping the slight embankment to get into position to fire at her. He was too slow, and he paid the price with a well-placed bullet in his chest. This was followed by a second round just for good measure. Quickly retracing her steps through the woods, she saw her driver heading down the road. She got in the car and drove in silence back to Ciudad Juarez. There was no feeling of remorse about the hit, as her target was one of those corrupt police officers who had aligned himself to a rival cartel to which he supplied information on the activities of the military in the area.

In reporting back to the cartel after the hit Avispa simply said. "Mission accomplished along with extras, you will soon hear about it in the news, although I suspect you already know." With that she went off to be alone.

The hit itself was an easy one and it went like clockwork, but she had much time to think about the other two targets. The thought that kept going through her head was that they had been sent to eliminate her after she had taken out the primary target. That thought left a very bitter taste in her mouth and played a major part in her next overly critical move.

It was time for her to move on.

Although Juanita had been recruited by the Juarez cartel, she considered herself a free agent and after her last experience she vowed that she would have no abiding loyalty to that or any other cartel. Dangerous as it was, she was on her own mission, a mission that motivated her and kept her going and anyone who came into her cross hairs was in for a quick exit into the next world.

It was not surprising then, that after a couple of years she became a gun for hire when there was a special job to be done. Her reputation was of such that all the cartels felt convinced that it was best to have her on their side, rather than against them. She was against all of them but what better way to get revenge than to be paid to take out those who she wanted dead in the first place.

CHAPTER 5

When Elan's bodyguard had boarded the private aircraft in Guatemala Juanita instinctively memorized the tail number. Now, with the assistance of one of her Ex-Marine Corp members who was now a member of the Bureau of Alcohol Tobacco and Firearms, popularly referred to as just ATF; she was able to get the name of the owner of the aircraft. In order to get the information from her friend without too many questions, she told him that while on a boat trip out to the Florida Cays early one morning a few days ago, the aircraft had flown unusually low over the boat she was in and she was very curious as it somehow brought to mind those stories she often heard about drug drops from aircraft. Her story went down well, and she got the desired information. It is always good to have contacts in the right places, at the right time.

The aircraft was registered to Manuel Ortiz, a Guatemalan and someone who was on the radar of the ATF as a possible drug trafficker. Not only was she given the information requested, but she was asked to get back in touch if she saw the aircraft again or picked up anything on the owner or his movements.

Her ATF contact could not begin to imagine how much she wanted to locate Manuel, but she could not divulge any more of her real reasons and intentions. It was all up to her from here on.

With the information on the aircraft in hand a simple plan was worked out, which if it went according to script, would lead eventually to Pablo. The plan was to start with the easiest to reach, and then work from there up to her main target. In her mind, the weakest link in this chain was likely to be Elias, so she decided to go after him first.

Using all her contacts in Mexico, she tracked Elias Gulern to the town of Corozal in Belize. Corazal is the district capital of Corozal, which is the northernmost district in Belize.

The city was founded in 1848 by refugees fleeing the Maya Indian uprising against the Spanish in the neighboring Yucatán peninsula of Mexico. Known as the War of the Castes (from the Spanish "castas" or race). It began as a war against the Spaniards, but because of the close relationship between the Mestizos and the Spaniards it eventually became a war against the Mestizos.

Nestled between two scenic rivers, the New River in the Orange Walk District and the Rio Hondo that forms a natural boundary between Belize and Mexico; Corozal Town is a convenient base from which to make short trips to the town of Chetumal, the capital of Mexico's southern state of Quintana Roo, which is nine miles away.

The city of Chetumal has a population larger than that of the entire country of Belize and is 20 minutes' drive down a rather bumpy road, or 5 minutes by boat from Consejo village near to Corozal Town. If you stand on the shore at Consejo, you can see Chetumal city quite clearly with the naked eye, about a mile across the water.

Elias could not have chosen a better location to hide out while he carried out his nefarious activities.

Corozal Town proper is easy going, unlike Chetumal City, its neighbour across the border. Corozal has devolved into a domiciliary town that is well maintained and well laid out. Apart from Belmopan, it is the only other municipal centre in Belize with reasonably wide streets and good drainage. This is mainly due to the reconstruction of the city, following its destruction by a hurricane in 1955.

The San Pedro Cay where Maurice and his friends had gone diving, is one of Belize's most popular destinations for scuba divers and snorkelers and is only fifteen minutes by air from Corozal airstrip. The distance by road from Belize City to Corozal is approximately ninety miles.

Lured by the Caribbean Sea and the low cost of housing, the area has attracted numerous expats, mostly from North America and Europe and has spawned large housing developments.

There is not much to do here and most of the activity takes place downtown around the Central Park on weekdays when folks come into town to do business. Weekends around Corozal are usually quiet, as this is used as a time to rest or to make excursions over to Chetumal where prices are more reasonable. The Corozal expats live a laid-back life, with year-round outdoor play, boating, hiking, swimming and diving.

The Corozal Free Zone operates as a minimal tax area providing casinos, hotels, shopping arcades and wholesale depots for many consumer items. Elias worked part time at one of the casinos, the Rams Head.

It was not easy for Elias Gulern to refuse to talk, based on the situation he had found himself in. He was securely tied to the center pole in the beach cottage he occupied. The design was meant to imitate a tropical island dwelling as much as possible. It was sturdily built of concrete, but the walls on the outside were then overlaid with the trunks of small trees, and the roof was covered with the branches of coconut palms. The floor was concrete and as if supporting the roof there was a steel pole in the center going from floor to roof. It was on this pole that Elias was tethered in a most demeaning manner. He was sitting on a stool with his hands behind him, circling the pole, where they were secured by a pair of handcuffs. His feet were tied together around the stool, so as to prevent excess movement and then placed in a metal bucket with water. To complete his situation, Juanita had taken the electric cord from the table lamp, stripped it and attached it to his left arm. The other end of the cord was plugged into the nearby wall socket and the flow of current was controlled by the switch on the cord, which once served the more innocent purpose of turning on and off the lamp. Juanita thought her improvised persuasion device was a bit crude but functional and would serve its purpose.

One of the skills she had learned from her father and older brothers from as early as age thirteen, was how to handle a boat and so she did not give a second thought to renting one and sailing the short distance from Chetumal in Mexico, to Corozal. On arriving in Corozal, she anchored at the marina, and early the next morning was on the move. Putting together her information on Elias. It was not long before she was able to identify where he stayed. Having done so she sailed across the bay and rented a cottage on a little bluff, just above the water's edge and along the dirt road that runs the whole length of the horseshoe shaped cove.

From the vantage point of the cottage, she had Elias' cottage under surveillance for almost half the day. She watched him as he came home earlier with a female on his motorcycle. They had disappeared inside for about an hour, then they had both left. Juanita mused to herself that whatever he and his female friend had been up to she hoped he had enjoyed it as she had plans for him later. Elias returned about an hour later, just as the sun was setting. He seemed in good spirit.

Juanita watched as he sat on a chair in front of the cottage and had a beer. Considering that she had not paid very much for the pair of binoculars she was using she felt very satisfied with its performance. Elias consumed his beer, then went inside. It was getting quite dark now.

It was time for her to make her move as she wanted to make her entry before he locked himself away for the night.

Juanita arrived at the cottage armed with a Glock 17 pistol, a pair of handcuffs, and a length of fine rope. Anything else that would be needed would have to be improvised from what she would find in the cottage. As she approached the cottage, she could hear the shower running and she thought cynically, "well you will at least die clean". Juanita crouched outside the window next to the rear door for a moment. Lady luck was on her side. The door was not locked, and she quietly let herself in. A quick glance around and she headed directly into the bathroom. Before he realized what was happening, she had pulled back the shower curtain and he was looking down the barrel of the Glock, complete with silencer. There was a moment of recognition, then he lunged at her pistol hand. Big mistake. She pulled back and shot him in the right shoulder. He fell back against the far wall of the bath and stared at her with a look of total shock on his face.

Juanita smiled a rather twisted smile at him, then ordered him out of the bath and marched him butt naked into the living room, where she secured him. With a bullet in his shoulder, arms cuffed behind and his feet tied and placed in a bucket of water; a new kind of terror was etched on his face. His panic had reached a climax as he watched her remove the electrical cord from the lamp in the corner. She slowly and deliberately stripped the two ends, then got behind him and although he could not see exactly what she was doing, his mind was alert enough to figure out what was happening. She was taping the two raw ends of the wire to his left arm.

With him now wired, Juanita started off by asking him who he worked for and if he had been in Guatemala recently. Despite his panicked state, he tried to put up some resistance to her initial questions but then she threw the switch and he convulsed at the electric shock which was amplified by his feet being submerged in the water. His female friend who had been there earlier with him would have been pleased to see the display of his manhood as it rose to the occasion in response to the voltage passing through him. After receiving three more jolts, he became more cooperative, and she promised him that he might not die that night.

Elias confessed that he worked for Manuel Ortiz. He also confessed that he was responsible for the death of Angel La Bron but that he did not blow up her car. She did not believe him. When asked about why Pablo was working with Manuel, he hesitated for a while and muttered something about bleeding to death. This was met by another jolt.

Eventually it came blurting out: Pablo was a member of the Gulf cartel but for some time now, he had been harboring ambitions of breaking away and starting his own group in Guatemala, away from the main areas of operation of the Gulf cartel. When he was approached by the head of the Gulf cartel to arrange the demise of Elan, he saw it as his golden opportunity. He figured that with Elan out of the way, he could now install and back Manuel in taking over operations in Guatemala, before anyone else rushed in to fill the void which was created, or before the Zetas cartel for which Elan worked, could replace him.

As Elias spoke, the pieces were quickly coming together. It was slowly dawning on her how she had been deliberately used to deflect attention from Pablo or the Gulf cartel. Angel was murdered to break the connection between her and anyone who might be traced back to Pablo and in the end, she was to be eliminated, before returning to the United States. Maurice's death was an unfortunate accident. The bomb had been meant for her. As for Elias, he had simply switched allegiance from the now very dead Elan to Manuel.

Elias could hardly have figured out what she had in mind when she gagged and blind folded him, before going to the front door to jerry rig a crude device with a box of matches. Nor could he see that she had casually walked over to the gas stove and had turned the gas on, just before letting herself out through the back door. About an hour later, there was a tremendous explosion and fire. She really did not care who it was that had triggered her contraption, they would simply be collateral damage. Elias was the first down, there would be others. And yes, she had lied to him that he might not die that night.

As she sailed back to Mexico, she thought about how Elias had begged for his life during her questioning him and it brought back memories of the stories of other murderers such as Elias, who when caught are often reduced to such cowards. She also reflected on herself and wondered what her reaction would be should she ever find herself in a similar position. Her thoughts, however, soon returned to mulling over all the information Elias had passed on about Pablo and Manuel. They would be next on the list. Pablo, however, would be the priority target. Elias had fingered him as the person behind the murder of her family and that single fact had propelled him to the top of her to-do list.

That bit of information had hit her with the force of a sledgehammer, causing her to momentarily shiver as his words penetrated the inner recesses of her brain.

Even as Juanita thought about her next move, she could not help but contemplate her own situation. It would already have been known to Pablo that she had not died in the explosion, and it would soon be known that Elias had been wasted in a most spectacular way. As these thoughts sank in, she realized that she would now be the priority target on Pablo's own hit list. With those thoughts resonating in her mind, she decided that despite her urgent desire to go after Pablo and Manuel it would be best if she allowed things to cool off somewhat and just disappeared for a while.

After mulling over it for two days, Juanita decided that she would fly to the British Virgin Islands and then slip out by boat to Antigua, after which she would fly to her destination, Jamaica. Juanita had enjoyed the tranquility and seclusion of the cottage at Blue Beyond in Portland and so she would head back there. She knew full well that it was a calculated risk, but it was one she was prepared to take. By going to the British Virgin Island and Antigua, she was hoping to buy as much time as possible before being tracked, if at all, to Jamaica.

She arrived at the Norman Manley International Airport in Kingston in the mid afternoon and headed for Blue Beyond by road. She was headed back onto the same road that had sent her heart pounding the first time she had traveled it. This time she was more prepared. Or so she thought.

Getting out of Kingston was quite a task as she was caught up in the midafternoon traffic. By the time she had cleared the city and was heading up into the mountains the sun was already setting. This, she soon became convinced, would be another experience in driving that would no doubt linger with her for a long time, if she survived.

Against all odds she arrived safely at Blue Beyond and immediately after checking in and doing her routine security checks she had two fingers of Appleton Rum, which was gleefully provided by the manager of the cottages.

The manager and owner was a retired bank manager. He was a jolly man who could almost pass as a clone of Angel La Bron in Guatemala who had met his untimely death at the hands of Pablo's henchmen.

He was eager to share stories about the island while sipping his Appleton rum. He knew many people from his previous job and his extensive travels around the island. In short, he was a wealth of knowledge and Juanita extracted as much as she could.

For the next two weeks she used the cottage as base, while she explored various parts of the island which reminded her more and more of her own homeland. In her explorations and sightseeing she carefully avoided the more populous tourist sites, sticking instead to the places not usually featured in the travel brochures but which offered spectacular scenery and above all else peace and quiet.

She visited Golden Eye, the former home of Ian Fleming who created the 007 James Bond character. Golden Eye is in the sleepy little town of Oracabessa, in the parish of St. Mary, on the north coast of the island. Oracabessa was named by the Spaniards who thought it possessed much gold. Their plans, however, did not come to fruition as the island was wrestled away from them by the British in 1655. The British kept the Spanish name, now translated to English, Golden Head.

The town later became one of the main ports in the island for the shipping of bananas to Europe. That activity was later moved to Port Antonio. The move greatly affected the large banana growers in the area and some of the smaller farmers. This blunder would soon see an area which was not previously involved in the cultivation or shipment of marijuana, now actively involved in the trade. Facilitating the trade was the Boscobel airstrip, which is located about a mile and a half from Golden Eye. In 2011 the airstrip was expanded and renamed the Ian Fleming International airport, catering mainly to private jets and other medium size aircraft.

The area next to Golden Eye is now a marina and recreational area known as James Bond Beach and Marina.

Juanita enjoyed the quiet atmosphere of the house and allowed herself the luxury of wondering about the life of Ian Fleming and what would have motivated him to create a character such as James Bond.

The following day, having returned to the parish of Portland where she was staying, she found herself admiring the famous Folly Ruins in Port Antonio. The ruin is that of a once opulent mansion built in 1905 by Alfred Mitchell, a retired mining engineer, for himself and his wife the Tiffany heiress, Annie Tiffany. The mansion was a very regal structure, having been fashioned off a Roman Villa and consisting of sixty rooms. Alfred died in 1911 but Annie continued to live there until the outbreak of World War One, after which she returned to the United States. Following her departure, the mansion began to fall into disrepair until it became merely a ruin.

The ruin was not the end of the mansion however, as it spawned a myth which is happily swallowed by persons who still tour the site. The myth is that the mansion was built by a rich American who had constructed it to impress his sweetheart and convince her to move to Jamaica to live with him.

It goes on to say that in the construction, some corners were cut and instead of mixing the cement with freshwater it was mixed with saltwater from the sea just below where it is perched. When his sweetheart came to inspect the property, it had already begun to crumble and she exclaimed "What a Folly" and flew back to America, never to return. The Folly Mansion was then left to crumble into the ruin which now exists.

Armed with her travel guide map she was truly beginning to relax and feel the part of a tourist. The life she led seemed so far away now as she pored over historical facts and side notes, while basking in the slow pace of life.

Her most adventurous trip was driving from Blue Beyond to Buff Bay, then over the mountains up to the Military Training Base at Newcastle, some four thousand feet above sea level and overlooking Kingston on the South of the island. From Kingston looking up, Newcastle looks like a large mural painted on the side of the mountain.

The base was built by the British during the early days of their occupation of the island. The climate at Newcastle was more like that of England and it was also much healthier than the plains below, which consisted of large areas of swamps where the yellow fever mosquitos abounded and caused many deaths amongst the English soldiers. The base is now the training centre for new recruits entering the Jamaican army.

Juanita stood for a long time at the side of the large parade square, watching a new batch of recruits being put through their paces and it brought back some bittersweet memories of her own training days at Paris Island Marine training base.

While lost in thought, she was approached by a young Captain who, in passing, must have noticed her keen interest and no doubt wondered what a woman by herself was doing so far off the beaten track. He stopped and after greeting her with a casual "Hi how are you?" went on to explain what was taking place on the square. When she told him, she had driven alone from Port Antonio, she could see that he was more than a bit surprised. Clearly impressed, he stared at her for a moment then said, "I can see you are a very adventurous lady". It was more a statement than a question and her rather feeble reply gave nothing away. "Yes, when I choose to be", she replied. The truth of the matter was that some parts of the road from

Port Antonio to Newcastle could have easily made the Khyber Pass between Afghanistan and Pakistan look like a walk in Central Park. The road from Port Antonio to Newcastle is probably one of the narrowest and most precipitous in the island as it twists and turns around the many ridges which make up the Blue Mountain range. Under the best of conditions, it would test the skill of the most competent driver. To compound the hazardous conditions, there are often numerous landslides caused by the heavy rains associated with that part of the island. They chatted amiably for a while longer, after which he invited her up to the Officer's Mess for lunch.

At lunch they were joined by two other officers and after dining they all sat on the veranda and continued the conversation. She told them about her time in the Marines, and that she now traveled quite a lot; skillfully avoiding going into any further details. She also strategically declined to have her picture taken, except with her own camera. She knew the pictures would be fabulous, as they had as background the entire city of Kingston, including the ports, the harbor and the Norman Manley Airport. She knew though that she could not risk them falling into the wrong hands, or worse, being posted on some social media site.

The officers talked her into spending the night at the Officers Mess and so after enjoying a most delightful supper, it was time to enjoy the panoramic view of the city below with its dazzling light show. It was breathtaking and to say she enjoyed every minute of it would be putting it mildly.

While enjoying the view of the city and enjoying the very cool, misty, climate with the air tinged with the smell of pine which grew luxuriantly on the surrounding hills her room was being prepared.

The officers mess was an old colonial building established by the British and so it came complete with fireplace and burnished brass knobs on doors and windows. The atmosphere was serene and seemed a world away from the rest of the island.

The bedroom was well appointed, and the bathroom was furnished with what had to be the largest bathtub she had ever seen.

The tub was half filled with water at just the right temperature to give her the perfect bath. She remained immersed in the tub until the water had almost lost all its warmth then she stepped out onto a beautiful red carpet. That night Juanita slept like a baby as the exhaustion and tension of the drive drained from her body and above all she felt safe.

The following morning, she joined the soldiers as they made their training run up to Catherine Peak, a towering peak overlooking the base. It was exhilarating to say the least, and she was incredibly happy that she had packed her running gears although she had no idea the opportunity to use them would have come about so unexpectedly.

Following her run, she had breakfast and then decided it was time to hit the road again, so she got out the map and looked over her intended route. It was decided to drive down to Kingston, then head East and follow the road along the coast, around the Eastern end of the island and back to Port Antonio.

The trip down from the base to Kingston was hardly less challenging than the drive from Port Antonio. The road was not any wider and was again just a series of sharp corners with what seemed to be bottomless drop-offs on one side and embankments on the next. Her heart was pounding the entire way down. On reaching the town of Papine which lies at the foot of the road from the camp Juanita pulled into a gas station to fill up her tank and to regain her composure. From Papine she headed into Kingston and was on her way to link up with the main road that would be her route back to Port Antonio.

Along the route she passed the sleepy town of Morant Bay and the courthouse where Paul Bogle, one of the National heroes of Jamaica, was tried and sentenced to death by the British who ruled the island at the time. Bogle had led a popular revolt against post slavery conditions in the island. A statue of him now stands proudly in front of the Court house. Leaving Morant Bay, she traveled Eastward crossing the Plantain Garden River, the only major river that does not follow the normal pattern of rivers in the island. While other rivers have their origin in the highlands, which form somewhat of a backbone to the island and flow either to the north or the south coast; the Plantain Garden deviates from that pattern. Starting on the southern flank of the Blue Mountain, it flows a short distance to the south then turns Eastward entering the sea near Holland Bay, a short distance from the Eastern most tip of the island at Morant Point.

As she continued to follow the main road along the northeastern coast, she could feel the gentle caress of the prevailing Northeast trade winds on the vehicle. One of the effects of the Northeast Trade Winds on this area, is that of creating one of the highest rainfalls in the world with an average of approximately one hundred and twenty inches of orographic rainfall per year, along the northeastern side of the Blue Mountain range and approximately two hundred inches on its peak. The wind was not extraordinarily strong but was still able to create moderate waves bedecked with their foamy white caps. A steady drizzle added to the overall, almost primordial sensation.

The result of this abundance of rainfall is that this region has some of the lushest vegetation in the island and an abundance of birds and other wildlife. Since 1988 there has even been a thriving deer population which, although not endemic to the island, is multiplying rapidly and has become somewhat of a nuisance to the farmers of the area. The deer were being reared in an area near the tourist attraction of Reach Falls but when the area was devastated by hurricane Gilbert they escaped into the surrounding hills and began to multiply. Another result of the abundant rainfall is the abundance of fruits and vegetables in the area. These were seen displayed in little stalls all along the side of the road, it was a rather marvelous display of nature's bounty.

Before reaching Port Antonio Juanita also passed the village of Boston, home of Boston Jerk pork; that very spicy Jamaican cuisine which is known worldwide. Though tempted to stop and make a purchase she resisted. She was a bit exhausted by the time she arrived back at Blue Beyond but that would be easily cured with a warm shower and a good night's sleep.

The two weeks she planned to stay were coming to an end rapidly and so she decided to visit the nearby Sommerset Waterfalls the following day, after which it would be time to say goodbye to Port Antonio and get back to a job yet to be completed.

CHAPTER 6

For the Mexican drug cartels to function successfully in any country, they must have persons on their payroll who reside, and have some level of influence in those countries. This normally includes politicians, civil servants and police, and in some cases the military.

Manuel, in anticipating certain moves and seeking to get a head start was in the island of Barbados where he had scheduled several meetings with a politician and other senior government officials.

Barbados was seen by Manuel as a potential transshipment point for drugs into Europe and he was making the necessary links with those who would be able to facilitate his business. He would have much preferred to be using Jamaica or Puerto Rico because of the numerous air and sea links but due to tightening law enforcement in those countries, he had decided to turn to Barbados.

Manuel also knew that the island is a popular tourist destination for visitors from The United Kingdom and Europe and this made it a prime target to be exploited. He figured that for the right price, he could probably buy a politician or senior government officer on the island.

Unbeknown to Manuel, with the assistance of her ATF friend, Juanita had tracked his flight to the island. She had also ascertained that he would be staying there for four days. That gave her ample time to get there before he left, and she was determined to make that his last trip in his earthly life.

Rather than flying directly from Orlando to Barbados, Juanita chose to fly instead to the island of Antigua from there she went by LIAT, the regional airline, to Barbados.

On preparing for the trip to Barbados, she had occasion to reflect on her good luck or the twist of fate that seemed to be working with her. During her conversations with the army officers at Newcastle in Jamaica, she had learnt that through joint training and disaster relief operations in the region, the Jamaican officers had developed certain links with their counter parts in Barbados. It was one of those links that she had exploited when she made a phone call to Jamaica and asked for a link with one of the Barbadian army officers. On a promise that she would look him up when next she was in the island, he got the information on where Manuel would be staying and passed it to her. On receiving the desired information, she smiled to herself and wondered how the provider had been so gullible as she had not told him exactly who had put her on to him and neither did she reveal her true name.

Manuel had booked a cottage on the East coast of Barbados in the area known as Bathsheba. The area was known for its foamy surf, which broke upon the rugged coastline as the tide was driven by the prevailing winds. The area was replete with cottages which were used by tourists and by some Bajans who spent their weekends there in their private cottages.

Manuel's cottage was just overlooking the fishing village that was occupied by several fishermen and their families.

Juanita occupied a cottage about fifty meters from Manuel's cottage. She had moved in during the night, a day after Manuel had arrived in Barbados and had moved into his cottage. From her cottage she planned her next move. So far things had gone according to plan. Her facilitator had chosen an ideal spot, and a quick check had confirmed that he had in position all the items that had been requested.

The facilitator had arrived a day early, made all the arrangements and was gone. He and Juanita were never to be in the same place at the same time. Knowing that she had a very tight time window in which to operate, her plan had to be meticulous and well thought out.

Juanita had one advantage over Manuel and that was the fact that she knew him, but he did not know her as she was confident, he had not seen her at the airport in Guatemala. Not wanting to take any chances however, she now wore a wig of very dark brown shoulder length hair which matched her complexion perfectly. It was a far cry from the exceptionally low hair style she had been wearing for the past few months. She did not leave the cottage all day, instead she monitored the movements of persons in the vicinity and in particular Manuel. He was observed when he left and when he returned to his cottage at about 6:00 p.m. that evening with another man. The other man left after about five minutes, after which Manuel went inside but emerged about fifteen minutes later with what appeared to be a glass in his hand. He sat in a large wicker chair and started sipping his drink.

Once she was satisfied that he was relatively settled, she left the cottage and headed out for a walk which would take her directly past Manuel's cottage. She was dressed in a simple Tee shirt, specially chosen to show off her ample breasts, and a matching pair of shorts which accentuated every curve in her well sculptured posterior. As she approached Manuel she threw him a casual wave and a "Hi how are you." Manuel immediately got up out of his bucket shaped wicker chair and returned the salutation, followed by "Are you staying around here?" She replied "yes" and continued walking. Feeling confident that he had taken the bait, she would now let him run with it. To let him swallow it even deeper she flashed him one of her most disarming and seductive smiles and said, "See you on the way back."

About twenty minutes later her way back, Manuel was still sitting in his chair, this time with a bottle of Scotch on a table next to him. On seeing her approach, he got up and enquired about her walk. "How was your walk, did you see anything interesting?" "It was most pleasant" she replied. He then suggested that he would be most happy if she would join him for a drink while she cooled off. Juanita accepted the invitation to join him but refused the drink with the excuse that she never drank while in training. She concocted a story that she was training for an upcoming marathon and that this evening she had done just a light workout, because she had been pushing herself really hard over the past few weeks.

They chatted for a while before Manuel confessed to her that he had an appointment in town, but he had enjoyed her company so much he was prepared to miss it if she would stay a while. She saw it as the perfect opening and went for it. The bait was now truly taken. "Why don't you give me a while to freshen up, then you can come over so we can continue our conversation." He gleefully agreed and she left.

Forty-five minutes later there was a knock on her door. On confirming that it was Manuel on the other side, she opened it with a drink in hand and what was more a statement than a question. "Its scotch isn't it" he was barely able to stutter the response "yes, scotch it is". She was standing in front of him with the glass in hand and dressed in nothing more than a see-through wrap. She ushered him in as casually as if she was wearing a business suit in downtown Miami. Manuel sat across from her, and it took a few seconds for him to compose himself, only to be thrown off balance every so often as she would provocatively cross and uncross her legs. His eyes lingered noticeably as he visually explored her inner thighs.

They spoke on several topics ranging from the economy in the United States, to the beauty of the Caribbean. All during the conversation she kept his glass topped up, as they snacked on an assortment of nuts.

At one point in their discourse, she went to the kitchen for a re-supply of ice and on re-entering the room, she casually released the top of the wrap which quickly opened to reveal her breasts and enough of her body to give Manual somewhat of an eyeful. It was too much for Manuel to handle; he started perspiring and had to resort to his bandana-type handkerchief to mop his brow and with a sheepish grin muttered almost inaudibly "this Caribbean heat." On seeing this Juanita knew in her mind that it was about to get much hotter for him and moved in for the kill. She walked over to him, kissed him lightly on the forehead then playfully took him by one ear and led him into the bedroom whispering "You, naughty little man I see that look in your eyes, well tonight is your lucky night I want to have that Caribbean experience too." In the room they both sat on the edge of the bed, then after a few seconds she playfully pushed him so he was now flat on his back and she got on top and sat astride him. He closed his eyes as she undid his shirt with one hand, while kissing him gently on his right ear. The kiss to the right ear was deliberate, as it blocked his vision, while her right hand extracted the syringe from under the towel on the side table.

The syringe was firmly driven into his carotid artery and the content of cyanide emptied before he had a chance to react. She continued to sit astride him, with the towel now pressed over his mouth as she whispered "Manuel, meet Juanita aka Avispa". She could see the glimmer of recognition as his eyes bulged for a moment, then glazed over. She continued to sit astride him for a moment then shook her head in a kind of satisfied disgust and got off him.

Manuel Ortiz was not as privileged as most of the other Caucasians in Guatemala. He grew up in a small rural village north of the Capital, Guatemala City. His father worked on one of the large farms in the area and his mother operated a small shop. Between both parents, they eked out a modest living for the six members of the family. Manuel, however, was not contented with the slow pace of life in the village, or the financial constraints of his situation and so at age fifteen he left home and headed into the City. He stayed with a cousin of his mother for a while, until he got a job running errands for a large manufacturing company involved in the production of craft items for the lucrative tourist trade.

With savings from his job, he purchased a small motorcycle and moved into a modest one-bedroom flat in one of the more depressed areas of the city. On one of his errands to a merchant in the craft markets he met another courier by the name of Antonio and soon they developed an extraordinarily strong friendship.

Manuel noticed that although Antonio did the same job as himself, he was always very well dressed in a variety of brand name items. He also had a large, relatively expensive 500 CC trail bike, which he would ride on his regular trips out into the countryside, especially on weekends and some week nights.

It was not long before Antonio confided in Manuel and told him that he was involved in the movement of drugs between suppliers and distributors. He then invited him to come along on his next run.

Manuel took up the invitation and soon he was also involved in the business. That was to be his introduction to a long life of crime and corruption.

Although having only elementary education, Manuel had a quick mind, and he learnt the trade very well and very quickly. Soon he was running his own distribution network which was cleverly fronted by several stalls in various craft markets around the city. Manuel was also a clever operator who simply eased into the trade without creating friction with others already involved. As his business grew, he began to purchase land and opened two petrol stations in Guatemala City. All this, by the time he had reached twenty-five years of age.

Contentment is never a word or a state that players in the drug trade embrace readily. They are usually propelled from one level to another by greed. Manuel was no different and soon he began to push against other players. This eventually led to him being regarded as a maverick and one to be watched. His name would soon be linked to the murder of at least three of the original players in the trade and although there were no hard evidence linking him to the murders, the suspicion was extraordinarily strong.

Manuel's activities were soon attracting the attention of larger players in the business, and one other ambitious player was becoming very interested in him.

Pablo Sanchez contacted him and was so impressed that he decided to fast-track his own ambitions. When, therefore, he was tasked to get rid of Elan, Pablo thought the gods had smiled on him.

Between Pablo's ambition and his own greed, Manuel was now left gasping for breath as his life ebbed away, almost in sync with the ebbing tide of this island he sought to target for his illicit trade. Target number two: Manuel Ortiz was now history.

At 11:30 p.m. Juanita was out the door and, in her vehicle, heading for another cottage on the other side of the island. From there she would depart early the next morning for Miami, then Orlando. As per arrangement, the cleaner would move in at midnight to get rid of the body and to sanitize the cottage. He would, unfortunately, have to cause a bit of collateral damage on his own when he got rid of the officer who had provided her with the information on Manuel.

CHAPTER 7

Armed with the information extracted from Elias, Juanita contacted the head of the Gulf cartel and arranged a meeting in Mexico City. She explained to him that she had urgent, critical information for him and the cartels' operations. She was very emphatic in conveying to him that under no condition should Pablo Sanchez be told of the meeting, as it had much to do with him and his operations. The cartel members were not particularly keen on the location set for the meeting but when she explained what was at stake and her own concerns, they relented. Xavier Morano, the cartel's number two man and three other cartel members were dispatched to meet with her. The meeting place was to be at a private dwelling in a residential area just outside the northern limit of the city, a short distance off the main north to south highway which enters the city from both ends. This area had recently become an area of conflict between smaller drug organizations seeking to carve out their own turf.

At the meeting Juanita explained how Pablo had double crossed her and the Gulf cartel. She mentioned that, under the guise of carrying out the cartel's bidding, his real objective was to establish his own organization in Guatemala and once established, he would break away from the Gulf cartel.

She outlined how Pablo had hired her to take out Elan and that she had carried out her task. On completion of her assigned task, however, she was herself targeted and almost killed on instruction from Pablo. She had been set up by Pablo and Manuel Ortiz, his associate and the person he had been courting to take over from Elan to do his bidding in Guatemala. On learning of this treacherous plan, she had gone after Manuel and Elias their hitman and had taken them both out. She explained that Elias was one of Elan's bodyguards but on the death of Elan had switched allegiance to work with Manuel.

Xavier listened in silence as Juanita outlined what had happened and although he said not a word, she could sense a feeling of admiration and acceptance. This intensified even more when she told the group how she had tracked them, and the methods used to dispatch them both. When he spoke for the first time, his words confirmed her feelings. He asked, "Why is it that you are not with us full time?" "You need to think about it." She gave one of her rare smiles under these circumstances and cautioned him that he should be careful what he wished for. To that response he rocked back in his chair and said "Santa Muerte! Now I have heard it all" and he called for drinks to be served.

"So, my dear Juanita why have you come to us and what are your expectations?" "Remember we are a very closed organization and as such we do not normally do or entertain outsiders." "Because of what we have heard of you, however, I decided to have audience with you." "So let me hear what you have in mind."

Juanita's simple response was. "I want Pablo Sanchez and I think I have earned the right to take him out personally."

"I also know that in taking him out I would be doing your cartel a favor as he is as much a pain to you as to me."

Her very blunt and forceful appeal struck a chord with Xavier and he agreed to her request, she was also promised all the information she required to assist her in tracking Pablo and carrying out her plan.

The meeting ended as abruptly as it had begun but as she was about to exit the house, Xavier quietly said to her "Avispa! Santa Muerte be with you." She smiled outwardly again but cringed on the inside as she wished him a safe journey back to his headquarters.

Juanita got out of Mexico as quickly as she could and headed for Orlando where she intended to spend a few days before being on the move again.

On her way home she mulled over the happenings of the past few weeks and was happy for the way things had gone. She concluded, however, that going after Pablo would be a much more difficult task and one that had to be approached with great caution.

As far as she was concerned, although Manuel had been in the illegal drug business for some time and had developed a reputation for eliminating his opponents, he had made the cardinal mistake of letting his guard down and being taken in by her seductive approach. For that he had paid the ultimate price. Elias was a street kid who had grown up tough and knew how to survive by aligning himself to anyone who needed his service. He was the typical muscle, more brawn than brain, but he had picked on the wrong target this time and he too had paid the price.

Juanita was right in her assessment that she had to exercise extreme caution in the way she planned to go after Pablo. She learnt later that as soon as she had left the meeting one of the men present had made a call to Pablo and had briefed him fully on what had transpired.

Pablo Sanchez was a former Captain in the Mexican Special forces and a particularly good tactician and planner of military style operations. He was well respected by his troops, and many followed him when he deserted to join Los Zetas; that deadly gang of well-trained, heavily armed military deserters. The gang initially joined up with the Gulf cartel as its armed enforcement wing. Once Zetas became strong enough however, it broke off and went on its own, eventually becoming the main nemesis of its former ally. The death of the Gulf cartel's leader and subsequent leadership struggles only served to facilitate this transition. When Zetas broke from Gulf, Pablo and several others remained. After a while, however, some of the original Zetas members who remained began to become wary of him. They thought he was becoming too ambitious and began avoiding him. That did not bother him however and he remained with Gulf and quietly continued his scheming with the assistance of some loyal followers.

On receiving the news about the meeting Pablo, who was in Mexico at the time, quickly left for Guatemala. From there, the following day, he headed to Venezuela and on to the island of Trinidad.

Pablo had, prior to that, received the news of the execution of Manuel and Elias and had decided that he needed somewhere and sometime to clear his head and to plan his next move.

While Pablo was heading south and into the Caribbean, Juanita was heading north, finally ending her journey on Vancouver Island in western Canada. She felt away from the maddening crowd and the climate was perfect. It was the ideal place for her to slow down the pace of her life and take some time out before returning to the planning of her next deadly mission which would be aimed at the dispatch of Pablo into the afterlife.

For the first week in Vancouver, Juanita followed a simple routine; she would leave her cottage every morning for a five-mile run, then back to coffee and fruits while catching up on the news. At about mid-morning she had a full breakfast complete with cereal and pancakes, eaten with a generous serving of genuine Canadian Maple syrup. After that, it was time to strategize until lunch time. Following lunch, it was time to relax, and catch up on the news again, then on to the nearby gym. After the gym, it would be out to supper. Juanita had made it somewhat of a ritual to visit a different restaurant each night; one night it might be Italian another it might be Chinese, Jamaican or Thai, she liked to sample different national dishes.

On her return from supper, it was either a good book or a movie on cable television, before retiring for the night. Under normal circumstances, this routine was so routine it would have driven her up a wall, but she decided to stick to it because she knew it would change soon and the pendulum would once more swing towards a level of excitement that most could not even imagine.

On the Friday morning of her first week, while out running, fate took a rather interesting turn; she was making her way up a slight incline when she thought she recognized a familiar figure running towards her. She quickly dismissed the thought. As he came closer, however, there was no mistaking it. She was looking at Kareem Earl, the young Captain from the Jamaican army whom she had met on her last trip to the island. When he saw her, the recognition was instantaneous and as they caught up to each other, they started chatting while still running on the spot. It was just too much of a coincidence, however, and soon they stood motionless in front of each other. After a few seconds he invited her to go with him to the little park on the opposite side of the street, so they could continue chatting.

Kareem told her that he had been in Vancouver for the past two weeks, attending a course in the disposal of hazardous material and firefighting. Then in a very disappointing tone, he told her that this was his last day, as he would be heading home tomorrow.

Juanita told him she was on vacation and would be there for a few more days. On hearing this, he wasted no time in inviting her to join him for dinner later, and she agreed.

He met her at their prearranged meeting spot, and they took a taxi to a Vietnamese restaurant in the center of town.

Over dinner they chatted about Jamaica and mused over what they would have put their chances at for running into each other again, so far away from home and so soon. They both agreed it would be an awfully long shot.

With dinner out of the way they decided to take a walk in the town. It was while slowly strolling along that she suddenly felt the urge to put her left arm around him and he reciprocated by putting his right arm around her waist. As he did, it was as if an unspoken message was sent, and they both instinctively turned towards each other. He looked deep into her eyes for a second then kissed her lightly on the lips, as if searching her mind for something. She tightened her grip around him and pulled him in closer. They both kissed with an urgency and passion that reverberated through their bodies as the passion of the moment swept them into another realm.

Without another word being said he hailed a taxi and soon they were on their way to her cottage.

That night they made love with such passion that the next morning, despite their superb physical condition they were two spent forces. She had released all the emotions pent up in her from her encounter with Maurice in Belize, combined with the tension of her recent exploits, the anxiety of the task ahead and the realization that this would be the last time she would be seeing Kareem, at least for a while. It had all come pouring out, and he reciprocated.

With a firm hug and a fiery kiss Kareem said goodbye the next morning and promised to stay in touch. She smiled and nodded in the affirmative. Her body was still throbbing from the excitement of the night before, she was enjoying it to the maximum and quietly wishing the feeling would never end.

The following week she changed her place of abode for another quiet area on the other side of town. She continued her usual routine, the exception being that she did not go out much at nights anymore and instead spent more time strategizing for the mission.

Her first challenge would be to get accurate, up to date information on Pablo as his whereabouts would significantly determine her approach and methodology. The cartel had promised to assist; however, she would not rely entirely on them and would employ other resources if necessary.

While Juanita was in Canada busy confronting the challenges ahead, Pablo was in Trinidad spending much time restlessly pacing his hotel room and devising his own strategy as to how he would rid himself of her once and for all. Like her, however, he first had to find her and he realized that might not be an easy task.

Both were now left with the realization that they would have to apply the well proven template applied to the conduct of an investigation; that is start at the beginning, collect your facts, plan and apply your strategy from the outside and work inwards toward the end of the mission.

On arrival in Trinidad Pablo contacted Carl Romnie, an old acquaintance from Mexico. Carl had been actively involved in bootlegging from Mexico to the United States for years but when the drug cartel came on the scene and tried to use his organization's network, he would have none of it. He closed his business and migrated to Trinidad where he opened a very upscale night club and casino. He was happy with his life and being married to a native Trinidadian and fathering two children; he was well accepted in the Island by persons from all strata of the society. It was, therefore, with an air of apprehension that he greeted Pablo when the latter walked into his casino in Port of Spain that night.

Pablo told Carl that he was on vacation in Trinidad and wanted to see as much of the island as possible. They reminisced about the old days but when Carl asked Pablo if he was still involved with the cartel, Pablo evaded the question. Instead, he diverted the conversation to enquiring about the government and politics in the island. When it was near closing time Pablo expressed his desire for them to stay in touch. "One day we could go for a drive out into the countryside or on a fishing trip for old times" he said. Carl told him that he was usually terribly busy but would see what could be arranged.

Carl was wrapped up in his own thoughts as he closed the casino that night and made his journey home. The last thing he needed now was some ghost from his past showing up on his doorstep and possibly ruining everything he had worked for over the years in putting his new life together. He knew very well that the cartels always had ulterior motives and he had no doubt that Pablo was lying about being on vacation. Had it been some other cartel member, he might not have been that concerned but Pablo was caused to be suspicious and cautious.

So, concerned was he that immediately on reaching home that night he made a phone call to Xavier in Mexico. He asked him if he knew what was going on with Pablo as he had suddenly appeared in Trinidad and had come calling on him. Xavier and Carl went way back to the days when Xavier was a young man and Carl had taken him into his business as a procurer of liquor to be shipped to the USA. Xavier had proven himself a reliable worker and had grown with the business. When the drug cartels came on the scene, however, he could not resist the pull to join up with them and eventually ended up with the Gulf cartel. In a show of gratitude, he was the one who had warned Carl that the cartel wanted to use his network to move drugs. He was also the one who had tipped him off when Carl had refused, and the cartel had planned to move against him.

Xavier, without going into too many details, explained why Pablo was there and advised Carl to keep clear of him as much as possible. At the same time, he should monitor his movements as best he could without jeopardizing his own safety. Carl made a mental note of what had been told to him and decided there and then that whatever it took, he would not allow this ghost to haunt him.

A week after Pablo arrived in Trinidad he was joined by Antonio Vargas and Brian Costello. Antonio was a member of Pablo's inner circle within the Gulf cartel and was fiercely loyal to him, while Brian was an associate of Pablo in Guatemala and a former coworker of Elias. It was he who had passed the information on to Elias and Manuel about Juanita's flight from Guatemala to Belize prior to the bombing of her vehicle.

The three men booked into a hotel in Port of Spain, the capital of the twin island state of Trinidad and Tobago and thereafter were always seen together. Such was their level of confidence that they would be safe on the island. Pablo had summoned them to join him in Trinidad and because he intended to involve them in his plans to deal with Juanita, he wanted them near at hand and ready to act when the time was right.

The plan outlined by Pablo to both men explained that his most urgent need was first to locate Juanita. He also intoned that he figured they would be just as interested in getting even with her because she had killed two mutual friends of theirs. She was the common thorn in the side of all three of them, and many others so they would find great pleasure in dealing with her. Were they to be successful, it would certainly boost their reputation amongst those they might want to impress with their capabilities.

While all this was going on, Juanita had made the decision to contact Xavier and find out if he had been able to get any information on Pablo and his present location. She could hardly contain the excitement which flooded her when she was told that Pablo had been spotted.

Her heart was pumping with excitement as Xavier went on to tell her that Pablo was booked into a hotel in Port of Spain with two of his cronies and from all indications it seemed they would be there for a while. After listening carefully to what Xavier had to say she thanked him for his assistance and asked him one more favor.

Four days after her conversation with Xavier she was back in Jamaica. This time she did not go to Blue Beyond, her favorite spot in Port Antonio, instead she booked into another cottage a short distance away.

The cottage was at the end of the road, on the same cliff as Blue Beyond. It had an upstairs room and a balcony but more than all it had a fantastic view of the Caribbean Sea and of the approach, parking area, and upstairs room of the main cottage at Blue Beyond.

At the same time, she was arriving in Jamaica, Pablo was receiving word that she was heading for Trinidad. He and his two associates began preparing an appropriate welcome for her. That evening, however, he received additional information that there was some confusion as to her destination and that she might be heading to Jamaica instead. That deception was carefully orchestrated to make him think she suspected he was there and that would be the reason for her going to Jamaica. Pablo was a quick thinker and planner, and those attributes would cause him to play directly into her hands, or so she hoped. When he received the last bit of information, he did a quick analysis and decided that he would leave Antonio and Brian back in Trinidad and would travel to Jamaica alone. He wanted to have all bases covered just in case she turned up in either island. Pablo further deduced that should she go to Jamaica he knew exactly where she would be. He figured she would be at Blue Beyond where they had met previously. At Blue Beyond he reasoned, she would be able to remain low keyed while planning her strategy against him and be able to strike out without warning, just like the wasp she was, when the time was right. It was indeed the ideal location.

Unknown to Pablo things were going strictly according to her plan. The favor she had asked Xavier was to disseminate to Pablo the false information about her travels and inform her as soon as he had left Trinidad.

Xavier in turn had got onto Carl and the plan was put in motion. Once the information had reached Pablo, Carl's task was to monitor his movement and report back to Xavier who in turn would relay the information to Juanita. Carl was in no way to expose himself by making any direct contact with Pablo, nor should he say anything about her that could alert him to anyone having the slightest knowledge of his plan.

Juanita figured that Pablo, in his zeal to be the one to finish her off, would come to Jamaica in person. She also figured that he would be looking for her at Blue Beyond because they had been there before, and he knew how secluded it was. What she did not anticipate, however, was that he would choose the same cottage she was now in, for the same reason she had chosen it, the excellent view of Blue Beyond. That small deviation almost impacted her overall plans in a dramatic way.

The four days head start Juanita had on Pablo had given her enough time to decide for her weapons and her cleaner to be in place. Her rifle of choice for this occasion was a 7.62 mm Mannlicher snipers' rifle and her side arm would be her trusted Glock 17, complete with silencer.

Having moved into the cottage at the end of the second day since her arrival in Jamaica, Juanita was, on the third night, in the process of checking her firing positions towards Blue Beyond when she saw the person coming along the track towards the cottage.

Despite the coming darkness she instantly recognized him; she recognized his well built physically fit body and his purposeful gait. It was for those features that on their first meeting she had mused that in another life she could have been attracted to him. Those thoughts were, however, only fleeting as they were competing heavily with the instant distrust, she had developed for him and which in the end proved her right. After what she had learnt from Elias, just the sight of him made her recoil in anger.

On seeing him, she had just enough time to retrieve the Glock that she had placed under the, seemingly casually tossed, newspaper on the kitchen table. She quickly slipped out the back door and waited.

Having the advantage of some knowledge of the surrounding area Juanita quickly surmised that Pablo had left the car in which he had traveled from Kingston, at the small, relatively unused, Ken Jones airport a few miles from the cottage. He would then walk out onto the main road and get a taxi. She further figured he got out of the taxi at the entrance to the road leading down to the cottages. She could see he was cleverly using the cover of the fast-approaching darkness to conceal his movement along the narrow tree-lined dirt road leading to his intended destination. She now realizes that it had been his intention to occupy the same cottage she was now in, ahead of her arrival and from there he would make his move against her in Blue Beyond when the time was right.

When he arrived at the cottage Juanita was standing as if glued to a side wall a few feet from the entrance door. She was dressed in jeans and a very loose-fitting T-shirt emblazoned with the words "Jamaica No Problem".

Pablo gently eased the door open and took two steps inside. Juanita appeared behind him with Glock in hand. There was instant recognition. He tried to close the door, but she was too quick for him and blocked it with her right foot while whirling around and ending up on the inside, next to him. He stepped away and despite the knapsack on his back delivered a withering round-house kick to her right side. The pistol went flying across the room as she blocked the blow. She in turn, followed up with a kick of her own to Pablo's midsection and a low sweep of his legs. As he recovered from the sweep, she sailed across the room in one diving motion, retrieved the pistol, turned and fired while still airborne. The bullet caught him in the groin, and he crumbled to the ground. He did not stay down for long but came lounging at her. Juanita moving like a cat, side stepped and hit him across the head with the pistol. He lost his balance and went down. Not wanting to finish him off just yet and not wanting to fire another shot, she used a nearby table lamp and whacked him across the head.

When Pablo recovered, he found his hands and feet bound, a gag in his mouth and his arch nemesis, Juanita, standing menacingly over him with a detached, cold look in her eyes. At that moment he knew he had a very short time left in this world, as he was a dead man.

Death, however, did not come so quickly. It was not until later in the complete darkness of the tropical night, that she had him hobble on one leg out of the cottage and to the edge of the cliff.

As he stood groggily with bewildered eyes, she reminded him of her parting words on their previous meeting "very pretty on the outside but this one is really sour on the inside". "Why did you think you could double cross me and live?" Before he could answer, she shot him and watched as he disappeared over the cliff into the darkness, towards the rocks and sea below.

Juanita made a phone call, then walked across to Blue Beyond where she had left the rental car. She got in and headed for Montego Bay where she would be flying out the next day to Orlando for some well needed rest and time for reflection. The Cleaner would take care of the rifle but the pistol she would keep for security on her journey to Montego Bay. It would then be permanently disposed of in the sea as she neared the airport.

The next week was one of memories and flashbacks for Juanita. She reflected on her childhood, on the things she had done and the direction in which her life was headed. Juanita concluded that she now wanted a permanent change of lifestyle. She wondered about that though and was haunted by the memories of those old Western movies where once you went down a certain path there would always be someone coming after you. Then one day, someone faster would catch up and a bullet would rush towards you with your name on it. She also found herself thinking about Kareem and their last meeting and it made her feel all good and womanly inside. It was an erotic experience that had left her wanting more and craving a life she had never really experienced before.

It was hardly surprising then, that after two weeks she could contain her feelings no longer. She made a phone call and two days later was picked up at the Norman Manley airport in Kingston by Kareem.

CHAPTER 8

After about a month in Jamaica hanging out with Kareem and checking out various business prospects, Juanita concluded that she wanted to open a business and remain on the island.

The next three months were spent travelling between Jamaica and Miami, putting the pieces together for the business venture.

She eventually opened the Golden Eye Dive Club in Oracabessa and operated out of the James Bond Marina; the business consisted of two specially equipped twenty-seven-foot Boston Whalers, very aptly named Golden Head 1 and Golden Head 2. She was incredibly pleased with her decision and how things had been going. Even so, she would still find herself thinking sometimes about Pablo's two other associates and whether she should have gone after them and closed that chapter completely. She resisted the thought, however, saying maybe one day she will and maybe she won't, but for now they can go on living. The other thing she wrestled with a lot and for which she had no answer was the way she felt about Kareem. Juanita had never been one to get romantically involved or even to feel so inclined. Yes, she had had close friends, but she had always drawn the line. Why then was she having these feelings, first for Maurice and now overwhelmingly for Kareem; was this just a new phase in her life that would end just as suddenly as it had begun or was it to be more permanent. Whatever the reason she was enjoying what was happening now; most of all she was happier than she could ever remember. She had Kareem whom she could count on without having to be looking over her shoulder and she had her business, which was going well.

The dive club catered for both tourists and locals, and she had entered into agreements with the hotels in the area to offer them special rates in exchange for them advertising her business. She and her team also offered dive classes to persons from the area, who were interested in becoming certified divers.

For accommodation she rented a villa about a mile and a half along the main road from the marina. It was on a cliff overlooking the sea, with a narrow set of stairs chiseled into the side of the cliff and leading down to the small beach below. The beach, though not much, was one of her favorite spots to unwind and just relax in its seclusion, especially when Kareem was around and not tied down with his duties. He was based in Kingston, but his duties took him all over the island.

Kareem and the pilots had spoilt her by doing low fly overs when she was at the marina so now, she would instinctively come up on deck and wave when she saw a military helicopter fly overhead. Sometimes they would fly over just to let her know that he was there. They would then head for the Ian Fleming Airport, where he would get off and cross the road to the cottage. There she would find him when she got home.

Although their relationship had blossomed into quite a romance and they were amazingly comfortable around each other, Juanita felt no obligation to let Kareem into her past and intended to keep it that way for as long as possible. In life however, nothing is guaranteed, and you just never know when your past will come back to haunt you. The key then is to be prepared just in case it does and deal with it as decisively as possible. Juanita's past was about to come knocking at her door.

She was working on some equipment down in the Golden Head 2 when her eyes caught sight of the two men walking towards the jetty where the boats were moored. They stopped to speak to Andy one of the locals who worked at the marina. She instantly recognized one to be Elias's associate whom she had seen when she had met Elan at the café in Guatemala. The other she could only imagine would be Pablo's other friend, Antonio Vargas.

On seeing them approach, she crouched out of sight while keeping an eye on them and reaching for the Glock pistol she always kept nearby. As she did, she noticed Andy gesticulating as if to say he did not know who they were talking about, then he pointed up the beach in a direction away from where she lived.

Juanita waited a while after the men had driven away then signaled Andy to come over. He told her that the men were asking for her, but he said he did not like how they looked, that he had a bad feeling about them, so he gave them a story and indicated that they could try the next beach further up the shoreline. With a promise that if he saw her, he would contact them, he was able to find out where they were staying. To reinforce his reliability and sincerity, he had warned them that it would cost them. They seemed happy with the arrangement and left while uttering "You are a good man. We will be counting on you".

Juanita did not like to live in suspense sitting there wondering when they would catch up with her, so she decided there and then to take it to them. She wanted to end it now and close this chapter before it got out of hand and began to affect or attract the attention of any other. To assist her in her scheme she solicited the help of Andy. He was instructed to discretely tip them off as to where she lived and suggest that they go by boat as they were more likely to find her down at the beach relaxing at nights until about 9:30 p.m. He suggested that the best time to go would be about 9:00 p.m. when it was quite dark. Her only other request was that he point out to her the boat they would be coming in so she could look out for it.

The following day Juanita discretely gathered all the equipment and material she would require. As it got dark dressed in a black wet suit, she made her way down to the beach behind the cottage. About fifteen minutes later she surfaced alongside the boat which was gently bobbing in shallow water near the shoreline at the fishing beach, a few hundred meters east of the marina. It took her only a short while using the skills acquired over the years, to have the boat rigged for its deadly journey.

About an hour later, both men died tragically in a boat explosion while at sea on what they had said was a fishing trip. The explosion shattered the peace of the normally tranquil little village and would become a mystery for the local police as they tried to figure out what could have happened. In the end they concluded that they must have been involved in the illegal practice of dynamiting fish, and something had gone awfully wrong.

Regardless of what anyone might think about the explosion, she vehemently reminded Andy that he was the only one people could connect with the boat and its rental and therefore for his own good he needed to keep his mouth shut and to say nothing about where they might have been going. Andy was more than willing to cooperate; he was no fool and he wanted to be around for a long time.

A year later, and after becoming comfortable in her cottage, Juanita was to be tested once more; two intruders using the cloak of darkness broke into the cottage. They were stealthily making their way towards Juanita's bedroom, when she suddenly appeared from behind the decorative oriental screen which partitioned the kitchen from the dining area. Before they could react, she opened fire and had no qualms about doing so, as they were in the sanctity of her home with guns drawn. Juanita did not do the normal double tap, which involves firing two quick shots at the same target but because there were two of them, she chose instead to apportion a single bullet to each target then repeated it before they even realized what was happening. Such was her skill and confidence in her aim. They both fell to the marble tile as one. She then walked calmly over, kicked their pistols away from their grasp and reached for her telephone to call the police.

The police listened to her account, and after doing their own preliminary checks, concluded that it was a case of self-defense.

It was not so much the fact that Juanita had sent the two intruders into the next world by violent means that baffled the police. It was something much more worrying.

What bothered the lawmen, was the seeming ethnicity of the intruders; they both appeared to be Hispanics and it was unusual in Jamaica for a home to be invaded by foreigners.

Although Juanita could understand their quandary, she kept silent as her mind began to wrap around her own theory as to what might be unfolding. Her past had caught up with her and this was the beginning of an entire new chapter.

EPILOGUE

In dispatching her two last targets by means of the boat explosion, Juanita had kept a promise she made to herself after she had shot Pablo. She had vowed that the shot she had used to dispatch him would be her last shot in this line of work and except in a case of self-defense, would not return to that means of violence. Unfortunately for the two intruders they fitted that description perfectly, they were intruders, and they were dealt with accordingly. She was satisfied that she had got her revenge and had also sent a clear message to the cartels. But then again, she would not allow herself to be lulled into complacency as she realized that in the same way she had been found by her two last victims, there might be others. She had to be ready. She was.

Printed in the United States
by Baker & Taylor Publisher Services